Fear of Blue Skies

JOHNS HOPKINS
Poetry and Fiction

John T. Irwin
GENERAL EDITOR

FEAR OF

···················· THE JOHNS HOPKINS UNIVERSITY PRESS

RICHARD BURGIN

BLUE SKIES

BALTIMORE AND LONDON

This book has been brought to publication with the generous
assistance of the G. Harry Pouder Fund.

07 06 05 04 03 02 01 00 99 98   5 4 3 2 1

The Johns Hopkins University Press
2715 North Charles Street
Baltimore, Maryland 21218-4319
The Johns Hopkins Press Ltd., London

Library of Congress Cataloging-in-Publication Data will be found
at the end of this book.
A catalog record for this book is available from the British Library.

ISBN 0-8018-5745-7

CONTENTS

FEAR OF BLUE SKIES

My Black
Rachmaninoff

I. The Unendurable Piano

Sooner or later if you stay in a place long enough something odd begins to happen to it. The walls or ceilings start to contort and parts of them may begin to look like tree branches in the wind or fingers trying to caress you. Or you'll start to hear sounds from the street you hadn't heard before, a whole range of curses and groans and repetitive laughter you thought you were too high up in the building to hear. You close your window and it seems to hiss at you. You close a door and it creaks like part of a haunted house.

In my case I began to hear a piano every day in the late afternoon or early evening, as if a music box had suddenly opened in my living room. The piano was more than faint but less than loud—certainly nothing I could complain about—and audible in every room of my apartment except the bathroom. The playing was very good, too, probably professional. Bits of Beethoven sonatas, Chopin nocturnes, and Rachmaninoff's Second Piano Concerto filtered down to me or up—I couldn't be sure. At first I remember thinking it would've driven me crazy six months ago. It was still too close to my divorce then and I couldn't bear to hear any music. At the very least I would've played some movies on my VCR (ones without painful soundtracks) that could drown out the piano, or more likely I'd have taken a walk as soon as the music started.

Now when I hear the piano, I'm just as apt to think of my father as my ex-husband, Ed. My father played oboe in the Philadelphia Symphony years ago and taught me how to play piano. I still have the upright Knabe he bought for me in my living room. But there are other times when the piano—particularly if it's playing the Rachmaninoff—makes me feel things about Ed, or even the big love of my life before him, that I'd rather not feel. When you hear the right music all the love ghosts from your past are liable to spring forth and make their claims on you no matter what you do to try to stop them. For instance, a week ago when the piano was getting to me I opened all the windows in my apartment to let the street noises in, but it didn't work. There could be an earthquake or a bomb exploding, and my ear would still go directly to a soft minor chord on the piano. It's as if I'm programmed to hear things that way.

II. MY TWO DOORMEN

The main doorman of my building is usually seated behind the counter in front of the mailboxes, at a dimly lit table, bent over a newspaper. Is he reading? Sleeping? It's impossible to tell. He wears thick, black sunglasses which perfectly disguise whatever he's thinking or doing. As a result I've never attempted to talk to him any more than I would risk disturbing anyone else who is sleeping or reading. Besides, he often isn't there; at least half the time he's missing from the lobby. I sometimes think he isn't really my doorman at all but some impostor who intermittently uses the lobby as his private lounge. There's something else bizarre about him. In addition to a uniform, complete with hat, he always wears a scarf high on his neck, regardless of how hot it is, so that almost none of his neck is visible.

"My Glenn Gould doorman," I dubbed him once when describing him to Ed. I still don't know if he's black, white, or Asian. Not that it matters, of course, but it's odd not to know.

With the main elevator man, who also functions as a doorman, it's very different. His skin is light coffee-colored and his straight hair is combed back in a pompadour and colored a dull reddish brown with golden highlights, as if part of a weird sunset had solidified on his head.

But in spite of all the ambiguous colors, Howard is definitely a black man and a good-looking one too. He's also as relentlessly polite as anyone I've ever seen in that kind of a job.

"Good morning" or "Good afternoon, Paula" he'll say to me each time I get on the elevator, flashing his even white teeth in what appears to be a completely authentic smile. When someone puts out that much it almost compels you to be polite back. So I'll ask him how he is, more often than not, and say thank you at the end of the ride. Then he'll say the most enthusiastic "You're welcome" I've ever heard—always with the same intonation and at the same louder-than-average volume, as if he's tape recorded himself and merely presses a button each time he says it.

So I began talking with Howard—obviously in brief installments— during our rides to and from the fifth floor where I live. I've learned that he loves classical music and chess and is much impressed that my father had been in the Philadelphia Symphony and still plays occasional gigs in Florida where he's retired. Howard is so knowledgeable about music that I've asked him if he plays any instrument; he said he plays piano some. I've wanted to ask him several times how he ended up at his job, but of course I never have. But I began to wonder about him, and when I'd see him working in the lobby at his doorman shift I was never quite sure if I enjoyed talking to him for a few minutes or not.

III. REVELATION IN A BATHTUB

The first day I began to think about my syndrome, which was also the first day that I really began to think, I was in my bathtub. I was following my usual routine and had allowed just the right amount of time to shave my legs, put on my makeup and clothes, and leave for work. I remember being still for a moment to listen for the piano and being relieved that I didn't hear it, then running a face cloth over the soap on my legs. Suddenly I began wondering why I was the kind of person I was, I mean why I had my particular beliefs and personality; then I wondered the same about other people. The only answer I had for this question, which I'd never really asked myself before, was a seamless programming that took place without a break from cradle to grave. A programming that my parents were only a small part of, because it was omnipresent and kept everyone focused on their syndrome (or if you want a more optimistic term for it—their lives). The programming covered all our thoughts, from our metaphysical system with its supposed heaven to our general political and racial views. It was so vast and had gone on for so long that even our authority figures, like our politicians, had programmed themselves without realizing it. In other words, no one was in charge and everyone was participating. It was an illusion, then, for me to think I thought my own thoughts or made my own decisions, about everything from the middle-management job I had in marketing to the kind of man I ended up marrying instead of, say, a cowboy from Wyoming or even Howard, the elevator man in my building.

I got out of the bathtub and began to dry myself off. I was shaking from more than the draft in my room. Society makes so much of our losing our sexual virginity, but I felt I had just had my first syndrome-free thoughts. I looked in the mirror and noticed a few gray hairs by my temples. I was thirty-four years old—it was to be expected. I thought, it's a good thing that we age or we'd have no awareness of time at all because we're programmed to block that out too. Then I thought about Ed and how he'd react if he knew what I was thinking. How he'd shake his head and probably feel sorry for me, thinking that I might be starting to lose it. I put my underclothes on, then finished dressing quietly. A few minutes later I was putting on my lipstick like a well-programmed slave. Good, I liked the irony. I could pose as a slave while secretly having my own first thoughts. I could embrace the contradiction for now and even find it oddly delicious.

IV. DISCOVERY IN A COFFEE HOUSE

The next morning I ignored the piano that started earlier than usual and reviewed my bathtub revelation. I even went into the bathroom again and closed the door to try to recreate it. Everything came back to me. My line of thought was wholly intact and still seemed clear and true. I felt so profoundly different inside that I looked at myself carefully in the mirror before leaving for work, but the face looking back at me was still mine.

The same soft hazel eyes, thinnish lips, slightly limp brown hair and close-to-button nose. A passably attractive face though certainly not a thinker's face, nor a rebel's.

At the office I avoided people more than usual and ate lunch by myself. On the one hand I was dying to tell someone about my revelation but I knew there was no one at work who'd understand. Then I started thinking about telling Ellen, my hairdresser, but all we ever talked about were men. We would meet for a drink or sometimes eat dinner together, and within two minutes the men talk would begin. I knew every detail of the woman's sex life and I guess she knew most of mine, but I couldn't picture telling her about this. I couldn't picture her understanding or being interested for more than a few seconds. The same was true with the other friends I had, with the possible exception of Etta, who I went to college with and who was now a paralegal and a frustrated writer of sorts. Etta and I would go to the movies and discuss the film afterwards or sometimes we'd go to a concert. With Etta I never discussed men. It was as if sex didn't exist when I talked with her. It was odd how specialized conversation was with people. Etta might be interested in what I'd have to say about my programming or she might not let herself feel anything about it at all. At any rate, I remembered that she was still on vacation in Paris, of all places, so it became a moot point.

I remember I didn't want to go back to my apartment right after work, and wound up, very uncharacteristically, at a coffee bar near Rittenhouse Square. It's impossible to overemphasize how popular these places have become in Philadelphia, where they seem to sprout up everywhere like wildflowers. I guess it's an inexpensive way to feel hip and maybe pick someone up in the process. I wasn't interested in either of those possibilities. I simply wanted to drink something and avoid my apartment for a while, especially since the piano was probably playing now. As soon as I sat down, I saw Howard, of all people, at the table next to me, reading a music review in the *Philadelphia Inquirer*. He lowered his paper, looked confused for a nanosecond when he first saw me, then flashed his smile at me with his white, impeccable teeth.

"Hello, Paula, how are you today?"

"Good, thanks," I said, with my standard perky voice. Well this was an awkward moment, but there was nothing to do but ask him if he'd like some company.

"Sure, yes I would Paula, thank you very much," he said, his face unusually animated even by Howard's standards as he began fixing up the table for me with more attention to detail than necessary. Normally I would have asked him about the music review he was reading, since music was what we mainly talked about, but for some reason, even though I considered his job to be a touchy subject, I asked him when his next shift began.

"I'm off for the rest of the day," he said, smiling, of course, without a trace of irony.

"Good for you," I said awkwardly.

The waitress came and I ordered my cappuccino. Howard opined that they made excellent cappuccino in the coffee house, and although I'd never been in the place before I agreed with him. It was as if by trying so hard to be harmonious and pleasant he unwittingly made you his ally, even if it meant lying about something silly, as I just had.

Then I asked him what he planned to do on his night off. He said he was going to stay home and listen to the radio broadcast of the Philadelphia Symphony. I felt touched for a second, felt like giving him the money so he could walk the few blocks down to the Academy of Music and attend the goddamned concert. He cared so much, he deserved that at least.

"Where's home?"

"Excuse me, Paula?" he said cupping a hand over his ear.

"Where do you live?"

"Oh, I'm sorry. I didn't understand you at first. I live in the Rittenhouse, right there in our building."

"Really? I never knew that."

"Yes, they give us special deals on the studios. It gets a little crowded now that I have my baby grand in there but I like it. Yes, I've been here a few months now."

Our eyes met and a strange feeling went through me. I began to ask Howard a number of more arcane musical questions and all his answers checked out. Then I felt a little ashamed. How racist of me to be so surprised that he could be a real classical pianist and live in my building. I quickly changed the subject, Howard remaining as friendly as ever, and twenty minutes later, after we'd both had our coffees, I excused myself and went back to my apartment.

There was no piano playing. I listened closely for several minutes—but there was nothing. The idea that began in the coffee shop continued inside me and was something I was sure of by night. The pianist I'd been listening to was Howard. It all fit, his recent acquisition of a used baby grand around the time I began hearing the piano (no upright could produce the sound I was hearing, especially the Rachmaninoff), and the silence I heard when I went back to my apartment because he was still in the coffee shop. In fact, it explained the long regular periods of silence I heard each day which seemed to coincide with his work schedule. When I thought more about it, I was pretty sure that a couple of times when I left my apartment while the piano was playing, Howard wasn't on his shift. Yes, it all fit and it was such a perfect irony that the best musician in the building and one of its brightest occupants was the building's black elevator operator. It made sense, too, that this would finally dawn on me only after my revelation about my syndrome, when I began to experience unprogrammed thoughts.

I had trouble sleeping that night. When I couldn't stand my TV any more I began to think about Howard. He loved music more than anyone I knew and was a better pianist than any man I knew also. He had a pianist's hands, too, with long, tapered fingers, and a handsome face, with large, soulful, hazel eyes. He was also tall and looked fairly well built. Why didn't I admit it to myself before? I was attracted to him. As I began to touch myself, I imagined it was his dark pianist's hands touching my body whose every part was now open to his fingers' touch—all 88 keys of me.

V. THE DIRTY TRUTH

Once you start to think differently you start to feel differently and you want different things in your life. Before I broke free from my syndrome, before I even realized the extent of my programming, it would never occur to me even to fantasize about Howard much less want to date him. The dirty truth is his race alone would have prevented me—not that I ever would have admitted that to anyone, including myself. As far as I was concerned I was very liberal on race issues and thought I had an impeccable position on civil rights. I got teary-eyed when I saw clips of Martin Luther King's speeches on TV. The same thing happened when I saw the movie *Malcolm X*, though I instinctively avoided the theaters and waited for the video on that one. I felt lots of admiration for Jesse Jackson, too, though I didn't end up voting for him when he ran for president, rationalizing that it would be a wasted vote since he wouldn't win anyway.

I was the same way on other issues. I thought interracial marriage was great and felt an inner glow every time I saw a mixed couple on the street or in a restaurant, but I, myself, had never dated a black man much less slept with one. No one ever told me not to, by the way. My family and early circle of friends were politically correct long before there was a term for it, but in a way, silently, my whole programming had told me not to and so I never "wanted" to, or even let myself consider it.

It was that way with my husband, too, who not surprisingly held roughly the same racial views as me. For instance there was this time during a long, rainy weekend that we mostly spent in bed having sex and drinking and talking very intimately about our pasts. It was a kind of erotic game we were playing where we asked and answered lots of questions about our pasts. I'd always sensed that he feared I'd once slept with a black man and wanted to know, and I, in turn, was curious if he'd ever had sex with a black woman. He went to a very liberal college so it certainly might have happened, but I also knew he'd protect himself by not asking that question—which he didn't—then or at any other time in our relationship.

So now I was wanting Howard. Now when I heard him playing Beethoven and Rachmaninoff, I felt angry, too, for the relentlessly affable Uncle Tom mask he had to wear in public while his playing showed the inner rage I knew he felt for his job in the building and for the double life he and other black people were forced to lead. My black Rachmaninoff, I said to myself while I lay in bed again and heard him playing. My big beautiful black Rachmaninoff.

It wasn't as easy to date Howard as I'd hoped. There were all kinds of logistical problems. For example, though I saw him every day it was always for ridiculously short periods of time in the elevator (our building has one of the very few hand-operated elevators in the city or the ride would be even shorter), or else in the lobby where he was often talking with the other doormen, including Glenn Gould doorman when he was around. How could I achieve the conversational breakthrough I wanted in a twelve-second ride to my floor?

Two things sustained me during this frustrating time. One was my conviction that I was a different person now, thinking new, unprogrammed thoughts, and so I didn't need to behave in the mousy, shrinking violet way I had in the past, always waiting for the man to be the aggressor. Given the way society had set things up, it was clear Howard could certainly never be the aggressor in this situation. It was wholly up to me.

The second thing was the anger I'd been feeling lately (admittedly a delayed hit) about my sex life with Ed, particularly the last half year of our marriage when, mainly to punish me, he'd barely touched me at all. Though I thought he'd probably been technically faithful to me while we were married, I wasn't thrilled that he had a virtual live-in girlfriend within a month of our divorce. I thought, given all that I went through— the weekends spent crying, sometimes even making my father or Ellen listen to it over the phone—that I had nothing to worry about with Howard who wasn't exactly an intimidating personality.

So one day when we got to my floor I asked him to hold the elevator for a second, and he said "Sure Paula."

I said, "You know I really enjoyed talking with you that time in the coffee house. Would you ever want to have a drink with me?"

"Yes, sure. I'd enjoy that, Paula. Thank you for suggesting that."

His smile was still intact but he looked a little away from me. Still he spoke in his typical accent-free, dialect-free, endlessly polite King's English, albeit a little faster than usual. Building Management must have flipped when they first interviewed this guy—the ultimate Uncle Tom—

actually better than an Uncle Tom, since he spoke just like a college-educated white man. Not that the other door and elevator men (except for Glenn Gould) weren't Tomish—they were. Or they acted that way when anyone white was around. I sometimes felt the buildings of Center City secretly financed a kind of Uncle Tom Academy to train these guys. They were so well-trained that I often wondered if they were acting at all, except that after the O.J. verdict I saw them slapping palms and high-fiving each other in the lobby. They were so carried away with glee then that for a few seconds they didn't care that I and a couple of other white people could hear them. Suddenly it was "motherfucker" this and "motherfucker" that. I thought it was refreshing at the time. Actually I thought it was glorious, though I don't recall my black Rachmaninoff being among them that dizzying afternoon.

"What time would be good for you?" I said to Howard.

"Oh any time would be fine—whenever I'm not working," he said with a little laugh.

"Why don't you give me your phone number?" and I handed him a pen and the back of my phone bill, and he wrote it, right there against the elevator wall.

"Thanks," I said, waving the envelope in the air as I walked down the hallway. "I'll call you soon." Thank God he didn't say his usual "You're welcome"!

Two days later I called him, and the night after that we had our date—only neither of us referred to it as one. We ended up going to a Center City coffee house again—a different one that stayed open at night. That was certainly as low-key as you could get, but at the time I thought it was the right way to proceed. I didn't want to scare him more than I thought he already was, because, say what you will, we were an interracial couple and he was essentially a servant in the building I lived in. I also didn't want him to have to spend any money or possibly embarrass him by offering to pay for myself. So all things considered the coffee house didn't seem such a bad idea, what with there being so many potentially awkward moments hovering around us. The fear of embarrassing him affected my conversation too. There was certainly no talk about the O.J. verdict or the Million Man March. I also sensed that he didn't want to talk about his past, either, and of course I didn't bring up his job or the few people in the building I vaguely knew. That left the inevitable topics of music and chess, the latter of which I knew nothing about, and my job, and a few general things like movies and the weather.

He was making a big effort, a Howard-sized effort to make things go smoothly, but he was also painfully tentative as if he wasn't sure exactly why we were together and was constantly looking for a sign that would suddenly explain it all. After an hour or so of this nonsense, I began to regret the way I'd played things. What was the point of being so careful if it only produced an atmosphere of anxiety and terminal ambiguity. Besides, I knew what I wanted to have happen with Howard, though I had no idea if he liked me or was even attracted to me. There was no reason then to play these tiring social games that I'd been conditioned to play my whole life.

It was a warm night in late October and I finally suggested that we go to the park across the street in Rittenhouse Square.

"That's a great idea," Howard said. Apparently he was just as eager to get out of the coffee house as I was. "I love Rittenhouse Park. It's like a touch of Europe in our city."

"Have you ever been to Europe?"

"No, I haven't been able to get there yet, but I still hope to," he said, with a sadder than usual smile. "Have you been over there?"

"Yes, a few times," I said softly, regretting that I'd brought it up. He began asking me about Paris and Rome and did I go to the opera house in Paris and in other European cities. Somehow I answered him, but I was simultaneously getting a major hit of pain remembering what had happened two days ago. I was taking a cab back from work then, looked out the window for a second, and saw Ed with an arm around his new girlfriend, both of them smiling as they walked down the street. By the time Howard and I sat down on a bench I was crying a little and had to turn my head away.

"Is there anything the matter, Paula?"

I didn't know what else to do, so I told him the truth about Ed, told him that every time I went outside I worried about seeing him since he lived only eight blocks from me, and how two days ago I'd seen him with the new woman he was sleeping with.

"I'm sorry, Paula; I hate to see you hurt like that."

I turned to look at him. His face looked kind but older than I'd noticed before, especially around his eyes, and I realized he was at least in his early or mid-forties.

"Thanks," I said. I touched his face for a moment and then kissed him, first on the cheek I'd been touching and then for a few seconds on his lips.

He didn't say anything. He looked a little surprised but said nothing.

"I like you Howard."

"I like you, too, Paula."

"Would you like to come to my place for dinner Friday night? I make a pretty good chicken."

"I'd love to."

"I have a piano, too. I'd love to hear you play."

Howard laughed. "Oh I don't know about that. I'm not much of a pianist. I'm afraid I'd disappoint you."

I was tempted to tell him how I'd been listening to him for weeks, admiring it and feeling moved and energized by it, but thought I'd better not confess that right away. I didn't want to come on any stronger than I already had.

VII. HOWARD'S END

It turned out I needed every one of the three days I had before our dinner. I had to go to the cleaners, buy the wine and some condoms, too (to be honest about it), cook the lemon chicken and mixed vegetables, and arrange to leave work early. I also had to give my apartment a thorough and much-needed cleaning. All this was nerve-wracking but not without its occasional rewards. While I was cleaning the living room, for example, I heard Howard practicing Rachmaninoff's Second again, playing it, I felt, with a little more ardor than usual. Was this due to my influence? It was certainly fun to think so.

I couldn't really think about anything else but Howard and the dinner during the days before it, and while he was practicing I sometimes felt he was divining my thoughts and responding to them in a kind of musical dialogue. That was more than fun. I couldn't remember the last time I'd felt so excited. I thought about calling Ellen and telling her about Howard, but then I remembered a couple of quasi-racist remarks she'd made once and I decided not to. I no longer knew what I really had in common with her, anyway. If things with Howard worked out I'd have to seriously reevaluate my friendship with her. Small matter. I was completely focused on him and felt convinced that, if there was ever going to be a breakthrough with us, it would happen the night of my dinner.

So he arrived, on time of course. I was wearing a black dress, a little low in front, with a simple string of pearls around my neck. Nothing shocking, but somewhat dramatic, nevertheless. Howard was wearing a navy blue blazer, gray well-pressed slacks, and a red tie. A little too preppy for my taste, but definitely a step up from the uniform. Also his hair was less outlandishly colored and slicked down than usual. For the first time it looked like hair I could touch and I liked that idea. Other than that he looked handsome, kept his opening polite speech of thanking me relatively under control, and, oh yes, he brought flowers, the dear!

He was less self-conscious this time, which I also liked, and made sensitive little comments about the different things I showed him in my apartment. When he saw a photograph of my father he asked when he played in the Symphony. "From '62 to '93," I said.

"Then he played under Ormandy as well as Muti."

"Yes."

"Those were great years," he said wistfully. "Great years. And there's your Knabe. That's a beautiful upright."

"My father gave it to me."

"Did he teach you how to play?"

"Yes." How did you know, I almost said.

"That must have been something, to study with a great musician in your house. Would you play for me some time?"

"I didn't keep up with it, Howard. I rarely play at all now. I play marketing games instead," I said, with a little laugh, more bitter than I intended. "Though I've been thinking lately of getting back to the piano, so who knows? Actually, I was going to ask you if you'd play for me tonight."

"Me?" Howard said, opening up his eyes wide and putting two long elegant fingers to his chest. "I don't want to ruin your dinner," he said laughing.

"That certainly wouldn't happen. Really, I'd love to hear you play anything at all."

"Are you serious?"

"Yes," I said. "You look a little worried."

"I'm no Horowitz, you know. I'm pretty much a beginner really."

"I'm sure you're being too modest."

"I don't know. Maybe later, O.K.?"

"Well, two shy pianists," I said, walking into the kitchen and arranging the food on the dining room table that was in the open space between the kitchen and living room.

Of course Howard offered to help, so I asked him to open the wine while I lit the tall red candle in the center of the table that I'd covered with a pink tablecloth.

Howard's table manners were impeccable and as I anticipated he was an effusive complimenter: "Lemon chicken! How did you know that was my favorite kind of chicken? Umm, the sauce is marvelous. Is that sauce homemade, Paula? Is it your own creation?"

"I plead guilty," I said, smiling from ear to ear.

"Well, you should patent it. A creation this exquisite should be shared with the world."

I started laughing, quasi-hysterically.

"I mean it, Paula. And you deserve to be recognized as a world-class chef."

I'll admit I had started the dinner still being ambivalent about whether I really wanted to have sex with Howard that night. Sex since my divorce had been quite intermittent and with generally poor results. But by the time he was through celebrating the joys of my salad and mixed vegetables, I had no more inner hesitation. I made sure I refilled his glass of wine and smiled at him again, more seductively this time, as we began my homemade peach pie. Howard praised that to the skies, too, but a moment later I had an image of Ed watching us. In my mind I was talking to him angrily about Howard, saying "He's not exactly your stereotype of the black urban savage, is he?" Ed was jealous as I exultantly delivered my cruel little speech—but then my pleasure faded and I felt guilty about how sad Ed looked and was suddenly sad myself.

I picked up my wine glass and looked away from Howard out the living room windows at the empty buildings across the street.

"Are you O.K.?" Howard said. My index finger went to my eye and I wiped away a couple of tears.

"You must think I'm a little nuts."

"Not at all. I think you're delightful and very talented."

"I just got a kind of flashback about my ex-husband."

"Oh."

"Maybe you think I'm a bit nutty about him, but not at all. I rarely think about him. So can we pretend this sort of sneak attack from the past never happened? 'Cause it rarely does anymore."

"O.K."

I was standing up now, though there were still pieces of pie left on both our plates. "Howard, could you just come into the living room with me?"

"Sure," he said, getting up from the table quickly.

"Could you just hold me for a moment?"

He looked at me searchingly and I found myself wondering if he'd done this kind of thing before with other white women tenants. I figured either way he would have to worry about losing his job, at the very least, since there was probably at least an unwritten rule about it, and then if one of the tenants was a bit off emotionally or mentally he'd have to worry about a rape charge, too, in a situation like this.

He put his hands on my shoulders. It was almost as if we were dancing. I suddenly wished we were. I bet he was good at it. Then I put my hand on his face and caressed his brown skin, and then on his hair which felt different—like an exotic plant—but the difference excited me and I started to kiss him, on his thick, curvaceous lips, until he finally opened his mouth for me. He tasted of my food and wine and also of mouthspray he must have used recently (the thoughtful Howard touch).

When we stopped I took his hand and said, "Come with me."

"Is this what you want, Paula?" he said softly.

"Yes, Howard, I want you. Isn't it what you want, too?"

"Oh, yes."

We walked toward my bedroom holding hands. There was not much light in the room, and I suddenly wished there was even less, just the reverse of the fantasies I'd had during the week when I imagined how lovely the contrasting colors of our bodies would look in the clear, full light of my room. Moreover, I began wishing I'd taken my wine glass with me into the room so I could have some more and couldn't help seeing it in my mind shining like some kind of over-sized jewel. I thought maybe I should just make up some excuse and go back to the kitchen and gulp down a glass or two. Perhaps it was my old, programmed wife-of-Ed self trying to sabotage me one more time from beyond the grave. At any rate, I decided I'd better start paying attention to Howard.

"You're so exciting to me," I said, not knowing if I meant it or not in that moment, although I'd certainly thought it before.

Howard said something softly in my ear about feeling blessed. I wasn't sure what he said because I tried to erase it as soon as he said it. I guess I was hoping for something less religious and more lustful, so I dropped the idea of talking with him in the bedroom. Instead I began to kiss him. I felt that, if he eventually got enough confidence, his true bedroom personality might emerge, and he'd leave his amenable but passive side behind and get a little domineering, which could be exciting. Also, I was feeling a little odd, simultaneously hyperconscious and absent, as if I needed to constantly be in physical contact with him lest I lose my own physical presence in the room and become weightless and invisible—a case for *The X-Files*.

We kissed for a long time and I felt a little like I did in the eighth grade when kissing was like screwing, the maximum thing you could do and there wasn't even a thought of doing anything beyond it. Except that it wasn't as exciting as it was then, of course, being fraught with the realization that we had to move on.

Come on, Paula, I finally said to myself, you're a new person now, thinking your first thoughts; you're not going to zone out like you've done with other men since Ed. Think about what you're doing. You're making love to someone you care about and want. You're making love to a black human being for the first time after feeling so much emotion toward them from a distance, a damnable distance your whole life, and now you have a chance to share your body and spirit, so you can't just zone out.

We began undressing each other, although I initiated it and wished he had. Programmed or not, I like to have the man start taking my clothes off first. It makes me feel wanted in a way I can't usually feel otherwise. Still, things were starting to improve; our kissing had passed through the stilted and pedestrian stages to a pretty sexy rhythm and undressing each other was more fun than not. I tried not to stare at his penis, thinking that it would be kind of a racist thing to do, but wound up sneaking in a look anyway. It looked more or less average-sized to me.

Come on, Paula, said my new internal voice, getting on my case again. Resist these stupid racist fantasies you've been conditioned to have, and experience this person, this artist, who happens to be black, who's gently touching your breasts with his long pianist's fingers, whose piano playing alone, that you listened to for so many days, shows he probably has more emotional range and depth than all the other men you've been to bed with combined.

We started sinking down to the bed together. He was moaning softly and started touching me, and I closed my eyes and saw the wine glass burst softly as if the glass were no stronger than a rain drop. For a few seconds, maybe more, I thought something radically different was going to happen—the physical compliment to my new consciousness—but then Howard began to very politely make love to me, as if he were painting me by the numbers, stopping methodically to ask me about how hard or fast he should do something, and I thought, alas, of how hard he tried each time to make the elevator land exactly even with my floor.

Then I felt bad for thinking that and told myself not to be so ambitious, that the first time it should be enough just to get through it. About ten minutes later he made a sweet musical kind of sound when he came, and I was glad to have given him a little pleasure.

"That felt wonderful, Paula. That was a privileged moment in my life," he said, lying next to me afterwards and stroking my hair. Ever considerate, he didn't ask if I came. I didn't—thus keeping my batting average a perfect 1,000 in not coming during intercourse for the last calendar year. Still, I didn't exactly regret that we'd done it. Things usually improve in that area in a relationship, until they get bad again. It was that way with Ed—though I didn't want to think about him now; that would be way too painful. So I snuggled next to Howard for a few minutes and it felt sweet, and my mind finally stopped racing, and I thought I might even get some sleep.

Then I felt him move. He was taking his condom off and a moment later excused himself to use the bathroom. My mind was blank at first until it occurred to me that I should put some clothes on before Howard returned. I heard the toilet flush—it makes a loud music of its own in my apartment—and merging with that sound a piano playing a poignant phrase from Rachmaninoff's Second. I felt a quick stab of pain or horror, and tears came to my eyes. So Howard wasn't the pianist; Howard wasn't my black Rachmaninoff. But, oddly, after the initial shock, I wasn't even that surprised. No, Howard wasn't an artist at all as I'd imagined; he was an elevator man. I couldn't say he hadn't warned me.

I began to feel ashamed of myself and started crying softly. Thank God he was still in the bathroom—no doubt making sure he smelled and tasted good for me. I'd better stop crying, I said to myself, quickly wiping away my tears. I certainly didn't want to talk about this with him.

Then a new anxiety went through me. What would I do if he wanted me again, because I suddenly knew I didn't. I couldn't do it again with him, and beyond that, what would I do if he wanted our relationship to continue? Obviously I'd done this for all the wrong reasons and should break it off. But if I did end it right away how could I bear to see him every day in the elevator? Would he continue to say his pseudo-cheerful "You're welcome" each time he opened the door for me, or would he not talk at all during the endless rides to my floor. Perhaps he'd tell the other doormen out of spite and they'd start hitting on me too. All these alternatives were hideous to think about. And every time I'd hear the piano, which apparently would be every day, it would be mocking me. It was all unbearable. I'd have to move out of the building as soon as possible, I could see that. Lose my deposit if necessary, but somehow leave within a week. I'd put myself in a ridiculous situation, a ridiculous trap, and there was nothing else to do.

I heard the bathroom door open and managed to get my bra and panties on just before he came back in the room. Taking his cue from me Howard turned discreetly away and put on his own underpants. When he turned around I looked at him closely. He was standing in front of my bed with a somewhat cryptic smile on his face, a slightly pot stomach, with his fleshy breasts hanging forlornly in front. A middle-aged body is usually a frightened-looking thing and his was no exception. There was a sadness in his eyes, too, and I thought that his smile was an instinctive camouflage—the way some animals and plants have protective coloration. Perhaps he sensed my disappointment, knew already this wouldn't happen again, but was damned if he knew what he should do or say next.

"Hear that music?" I suddenly blurted.

"Yes, the Rachmaninoff Second. Beautiful piece. A Korean girl on the fourth floor plays that. She's a student at Curtis who moved in a few months ago. She's very talented, isn't she? God, I'd give anything to play like that."

Yes, Howard would know all about the pianists in the building. The building was his theater and concert hall and museum. The building was his Europe. Then I got an idea. "Will you sit down and listen to it with me for awhile?" I said, as I put on my dress.

"Sure Paula," he said, sitting on the bed without touching me. We began listening to the music silently and I thought that he very well might know now that the romantic part of our relationship was over, but unless he said something himself at some point, which he probably wouldn't, I'd have to make it clear in a way that wouldn't hurt him too much. It would be dreadful, but I'd have to do it.

We kept listening, longer than I thought we would. I began to picture the Korean girl who practiced these phrases over and over every day so that one day they might sound new and spontaneous. That was a kind of love, and I wondered what the source of passion was in her life that allowed her to do it. I stole another glance at Howard. For a moment I felt his loneliness, his disappointment over much more than this night, and I thought that some time in the future we might go to a concert together as friends, perhaps a piano recital at Curtis like the one the Korean girl was preparing for. Then a voice inside me said, you're still deluding yourself you foolish woman, you'll never get over your embarrassment and shame enough to do that. But later I felt maybe I would, that maybe the concert was really the first thought of my new life or at least the first one that made sense.

Fear of Blue Skies

Martin used to count on his fingers the number of things his father had done alone with him. They had seen a movie together called *The Wrong Man;* they had played Monopoly three times. He thought they'd run around the house when he was very young. They definitely played miniature golf once and went swimming together a few times, and once they drove from Newport to Boston to see the Red Sox play, but it was an extra-inning game and they had to leave before the game was over. The experience of being alone with his father was always dramatic, and Martin would spend much of their time together observing him almost with dispassion so as not to miss or falsify a thing. But once after his father sank a long putt, Martin blurted out, "You're the Babe Ruth of miniature golf," and his astonished father smiled.

As he got older these events happened less often and Martin noticed that his father was drinking a lot and that his drinking made him even more remote, if also more deferential toward Martin's mother. Drinking had quite a different effect on her. Reticent or aloof most of the time, she would break into a tirade about some minute slight from her social circle, or some annoying habit of her husband's, that often ended with her weeping and Martin futilely trying to comfort her on the living room couch. It was as if an actress in a silent movie suddenly broke into hysterical speech for thirty minutes. Then after the alcohol wore off, she would fall back into the silent film again.

Martin was polite but reserved with his classmates, most of whom considered him nice enough but dull. He was aware that he was lucky to be rich without being openly resented by his less wealthy classmates and was content to stay in the background. When they played baseball or basketball he was sometimes asked to umpire because his classmates respected his impartiality and perhaps, even, his honor. That pleased Martin, who was not a talented player but enjoyed watching them play and took his role seriously.

· · · · · · · · · ·

Shortly before his twelfth birthday, Martin had a dream which recurred with slight variations throughout his adolescence. He was outside refereeing his classmates' basketball game. The sun was shining strongly in a cloudless blue sky. Suddenly, he began to feel weightless and rose from the playground balloon-like, higher and higher into the sky. At the point when he began to become transparent and it appeared he would merge with the sky, he'd wake up frightened or sad.

At first he wanted to tell his parents about the nightmare, but they were sleeping in separate rooms by then, which created a problem since he wanted them to be together when he told them. He thought about going to one of them and asking them to accompany him to the other parent's room, but it seemed in the final analysis too unlikely. Whenever he had the dream he knew he could never get back to sleep that night, so his chief fear became his dream of the bright azure sky that seemed to swallow his weight and drain him of color.

Martin's parents didn't worry much about him, although as he got older they wished he were more ambitious. But since both of them had inherited their wealth and neither had a career anymore, they didn't feel they could talk to Martin authoritatively about his mediocre grades and passive attitude toward his future. It was enough for them that he was a well-mannered young man who would probably grow up to be quite attractive, as he was tall, had clear green eyes, and was a fastidious dresser. Moreover, he didn't drink at all and he did manage to get into an accredited college where he received a steady stream of C's. It was assumed that he would go to some kind of business school after he graduated from college and had taken a year off to travel, for by then he would have received the first fifty-thousand dollars of a trust fund from his maternal grandfather.

It was during Martin's senior year at college, when he turned twenty-two, that he began to concentrate on just what he would do with the money. He decided that he wouldn't use it to travel through Europe, as his mother suggested, but to find a new home, a place where he could meet different people and perhaps become different himself. New York City seemed a logical place, and as soon as Martin graduated, collected his "reward money" as he thought of it, and said his rather muted good-byes to his parents, he moved there, renting a one-bedroom apartment on the Upper West side.

But he'd miscalculated his capacity to adapt. The pace was too fast for him, the crowds too big and impatient like nothing he could have imagined, and he began to have trouble sleeping. One night he had his blue sky dream and his father was one of the basketball players. His pencil mustache and toothy white smile were the last things Martin saw before he started his ascent in the sky.

When he couldn't sleep he'd try remembering his favorite moments from childhood, like the miniature golf game with his father, but they no longer seemed clear enough to recall or believe in as actual memories. Instead he'd find himself listening to the sounds of the city—random noises that seeped through his shut windows and scattered like insects. Martin very quickly became convinced he'd never sleep well, if at all, in New York and decided he had to move. But where? What he realized he wanted was to be near a friendly group of people, and he thought his chances would be better where the weather was warmer. He eliminated Miami Beach as having too many of the negative qualities of New York, but grew increasingly excited the more he read about California. Soon he supplemented his reading by watching as many movies or TV shows about it as he could. After a couple of more weeks he decided that California represented his best chance, and immediately he began trying to sublet his apartment. While that was being settled he thought carefully about what part of the state to move to before choosing a picturesque resort town eighty miles north of Los Angeles, named Santa Vista.

As soon as he got off the plane he rented a Toyota (which he eventually bought) and started driving through his new town. Martin was stunned by Santa Vista's beauty. With its backdrop of mountains, its palm trees on the beaches, and its exotic birds and flowers on every street, he felt its nickname of Paradise was scarcely exaggerated. The people of Santa Vista were unusually attractive, too, and not just the students at the university. Everyone around him seemed lean and fit—even Santa Vistan women in their sixties were still alluring.

There was something else he appreciated about the town, even more than its physical beauty. He felt a spirit of toleration in Santa Vista, a sense that he could look and behave the way he wanted without being judged deficient or even attracting attention.

After staying in a hotel for a few weeks, he rented a modest apartment whose flower-filled courtyards he grew to love. So far he had made no effort to make friends, but wasn't aware of wanting any. He enjoyed being alone and knowing that the spirit of the town was always around him. Shortly, he established a comfortable routine. He'd have breakfast at Audrey's where the working people of the town ate. He liked seeing the bus drivers and maintenance men before they went to work; their talk about sports, their loud laughter, even their cigarette smoke—a rarity in a Santa Vista restaurant—didn't bother him. In fact, it reassured him in a way he couldn't have explained. Sometimes when he wanted to be near older people, whom he also found comforting, he'd walk up State Street and have breakfast at the Copper Coffee Pot, a cafeteria that catered to residents from the senior citizen homes in the foothills.

After breakfast he tried to read for an hour, not wanting his mind to go slack now that he was out of college; then he'd walk into town and try to spend some time on his finances. He still didn't find it interesting but realized it was important to keep informed. He knew if he were prudent he might stretch his time out to two years before he'd have to get a job, and that, of course, was reassuring.

Generally, he had lunch at either the Presidio or The Bakery. The food was excellent at both places and so was the view of the mountains. Sometimes during lunch he wrote postcards to his parents. After lunch he'd walk down State Street two miles until he reached the town beach. There he'd walk left along the beach, spreading out his towel near a group of people—men as often as women—and listening to their conversation. He was not hoping to join them nor was he listening to the details of their lives. It was that Santa Vistan tone he wanted to hear wafting up to him on a light wind, reminding him that things were going smoothly in his town. Once the people he listened to were lovers so the tone was even sweeter, and he wound up listening to them for hours.

That night Martin dreamt he was alone on the beach flying a blue kite. He ran up and down a series of sand dunes, the kite a hundred feet up in the blue sky. Then suddenly the beach flattened, the dunes disappeared. When he looked again he was in the air a hundred feet or higher in a sky of chalk. The kite, which was now also white, had tricked him. Held down by a heavy rock, it was flying him.

Martin woke up trembling. It was more frightening than the basketball dream, and after thinking about it, Martin decided he needed more human contact in his nights. No longer would he cook for himself; instead he would go out to Chez Charlotte where there were exquisite chicken crepes and some of the most glamorous people in Santa Vista eating them, or else to the Copper Coffee Pot where he could listen to the old people. Then he'd rent a new movie each night to play on his VCR before falling asleep.

For a week his new schedule worked well, until the afternoon when he sat near two lovers on the beach again. This time he looked at them long enough to see they were both blond—he in a white bikini, she in one of those light brown suits that only covered her nipples and the dividing line of her rear end. Apparently oblivious to Martin, who was less than ten feet away, they were talking in normal voices about the things they were going to do to each other in bed as soon as they got home.

On his way home that day Martin worried about not sleeping, which would inevitably mean late-night memories (or attempts at memories) of his old life in Newport. Martin decided to help his chances by going to the video store and renting one of his favorite movies, *Starting Over*, that he'd seen perhaps fifteen times. It was a Burt Reynolds comedy—his best movie, in Martin's opinion—about a fortyish man who unexpectedly falls in love again shortly after his divorce. It had a very happy ending.

Martin made some popcorn and lemonade to have during the movie, but when it ended he still wasn't tired so he turned on TV. There were a number of adult phone ads on, and he found himself transfixed by the woman on the "Hot Talk" ad who invited people to call her anytime by a swimming pool where she wasn't wearing much more than the blonde woman he'd seen that afternoon on the beach. When he eventually closed his eyes he saw a kind of composite image of the woman in the phone ad and the woman on the beach shimmering in front of him, making it impossible to sleep. He thought it was because he hadn't had sex with anyone in so long; in fact, in his whole life he'd done it only twice. Each time it was with a woman from an escort service who'd come to his home while his parents were away visiting relatives. On a Friday night, shortly before Martin's own trip to New York, he had called the service and done it for the first time, after several false starts, with one woman, and the next night, still alone in the house, he'd called the service again and slept with a second woman.

Now he decided he couldn't wait any longer. But the situation was complicated since as far as he knew Santa Vista had no prostitutes—indeed, it didn't even have a slum. That meant he'd have to go to L.A., which he dreaded, and do it there. But with no chance of sleep there was little point in postponing things, so Martin got in his Toyota and drove to Los Angeles, finally stopping to check in at a Motel 6 in Hollywood.

He started walking around Sunset Boulevard but discovered the prostitutes there were suspicious of pedestrians, and after one openly accused him of being a cop he went to his car and finally picked up a woman who approached him. She was a blonde of indeterminate age, named Candy, who wore a ridiculously short pink skirt. She tried to talk him into doing it in the car (no doubt so she could get out on the street faster), but Martin insisted on the motel room. He wanted to simulate, as much as possible, what he imagined a normal couple would do.

After it was over it seemed to be something that his body had done automatically, like drinking a glass of water, and he figured that Candy probably felt the same way, though she was kind enough to pretend it was much more exciting than that—and pretend so well that he couldn't actually be sure how much she'd enjoyed it.

"Hey, you look like you're trying to figure out if you had a good time or not," she said, as she was putting on her pink quasi-transparent bra.

Martin turned away and blushed slightly. "I had a wonderful time." Then he handed her an extra ten dollars, which won him a compliment, as she immediately put it in an opening in her stockings.

"Where will you be tomorrow night?" he said.

"Same place, same corner. Hope I see you there."

But when he returned the next night she wasn't there. He waited until 1:30, then picked up a black woman named Valerie. She wore a bright red dress but seemed tired, and Martin thought she was probably on some drug. He took her to the same room in Motel 6 he'd used the night before and began to undress.

"What you want, man?" she said, standing in her outfit by the door like a guard at a movie turnstile.

Martin shrugged, "Just the regular."

"Regular what? You want to screw me, mister?"

"Yes," he said softly.

"Then pay me now. You got to pay me 'fore I take my clothes off, see? That's fifty bucks, mister."

It had been different with Candy, but Martin complied. While they were in bed he tried to kiss Valerie, but she turned her head away.

"Mister, I don't kiss clients. Just keep grinding an' you'll be done soon."

It was funny, her eyes looked tired, but her voice was strong. Martin closed his own eyes, did what she said, and thanked her when it was over.

Once in his car he thought how doubly absurd it was that she should feel nothing, too. He was on the highway heading back to Santa Vista thinking that the whole world of hookers and their clients was a web of illusion spun out over and over by the mutually addicted. He passed Malibu and Carpinteria. He noticed the stars were shining over the water. Then, as if his dream were happening to him while he was awake, he started to feel his weight leaving him, and he pulled over to the soft shoulder as fast as he could. Why was this happening to him? What did it mean? He tried to remember Candy, as if that might help him feel his body, but he couldn't, nor could he recall anything but the most fleeting image of Valerie. He closed his eyes, gripping the steering wheel for support, and saw an image of his stiff corpse-like father drinking and his mother crying on the couch. Was it because of them? But at least they had provided for him in some sense, he thought, whereas he paid only for his own existence, since he had no one else in it, of course. Maybe it was wrong to look to the past for help. Perhaps he should direct everything toward the future and do something worthwhile in Santa Vista. But when he thought of the town with its restaurants and banks and shining harbor he was afraid he would remain weightless there as well.

While he stayed parked gripping the wheel, cars whizzed by him, their lights roaring away from L.A. Martin's thoughts returned to the streets and the prostitutes. He had gone there for pleasure but his whole purpose may have been wrong. Gradually he got an idea about what he could do differently and how Santa Vista could still be put to good use. As he thought about it his weight slowly returned to him, it seemed about a pound per second. By the time his idea had become a conviction he felt solid, and he turned his car around and drove back to Hollywood.

· · · · · · · · · ·

He backed up and headed down another side street off Sunset Boulevard. How many had turned him down? Five? Six? He'd have to be more emphatic in his approach next time. He turned onto Hollywood Boulevard. For fifteen minutes there was no one, just the lights coming out of the dark.

Then he pulled up beside a skinny blonde wearing a half-buttoned red jump suit so bright her pale face seemed to almost disappear.

"Can I talk to you?"

"What about?"

He thought she couldn't be older than sixteen, despite her heavy makeup, and maybe was younger than that.

"How'd you like to get out of here?"

"Depends. How much you got to spend?"

"I have a home in Santa Vista where you can stay."

"My meter says that's about one-fifty."

"You don't understand."

"Oh, really?"

"I'm offering you my apartment to live in."

"Great. Can I sell it?"

"I don't want anything in return."

"You into kidnapping? That's very expensive."

"I'm trying to help you. Really. Give you a chance to get off the street and start a new life."

For a moment she looked at him quizzically. The rest of her face had disappeared so he only saw her two green eyes that sparkled unnaturally.

"Yeah, well thanks, but no thanks," she said walking away from his car. He watched her moving ghost-like down the dark block, then opened his car door and yelled, "You'll die if you stay on the streets, you'll get AIDS and die."

"I'll die sooner if I stay with you," came the disembodied reply.

"Jesus Christ," he hissed and pounded his fist on the dashboard.

He drove down the rest of the block, saw no one, got onto Sunset, and drove down it a few miles and began to think that maybe it was too late now. He passed Hollywood High School and had slowed down to look at it, when a girl with a desperate face suddenly knocked on his window signaling him to let her in. Martin immediately opened the door. She was wearing a black miniskirt and a gold silk shirt tied together in a knot to hide a bad rip. She had long, fluffed-out, black hair and large eyes that looked frightened and were badly streaked with makeup.

"Start driving, okay?"

"What's the matter?" he said, but the girl was twisted around in her seat looking out the rear window and didn't answer him. Martin drove down Sunset looking for the exit that would lead to Santa Vista.

He drove a couple of miles without talking or even looking at the girl, who was still periodically staring at the road behind him.

"You wanna date?" she said, finally turning around and half looking at him.

"No, thanks."

"Mind if I just ride with you a few more miles, maybe you'll change your mind."

"Sure, you can ride. I'm going to Santa Vista."

She didn't answer him. She was fidgeting with her shirt, then with her makeup.

"You in some kind of trouble?"

"Yeah, you could say that."

"Somebody after you?"

"Maybe. Yeah, somebody just tried to break my bones actually. So you want a date or what?"

Martin sneaked a look at her and noticed a cut below her left eye that she'd tried to camouflage with makeup.

"No, I don't want a date."

"Great. Are you a cop? Tell me you're a cop, it'll make my night complete."

Martin smiled. "I'm not a cop." He had turned off the exit and was now on the highway heading north.

"Well, thanks for the ride, but how about letting me out now?"

"I'm on a highway. I can't let you out on the highway."

"Sure you can."

"Is that what you want?"

"I don't want to fight you, okay. I just had one, you know? I don't want trouble. Just let me out of the fucking car, okay?"

"Calm down, will you?"

"It's not about calming down. It's about me getting out of the fucking car."

"You have to calm down first and talk to me for a couple of minutes, that's all I ask."

"Talk is free, ain't it? I don't like free."

"Don't worry. I'll give you money. I've got cash."

"I already asked you if you wanted a date."

"You're missing the point. You came to me. You made a decision to put me in your life."

"Okay. You did me a favor." She turned to him and pretended to assess his looks. "You're kind of cute. I'll give you half price."

"You're still missing the point."

"There is no point. What, you want it free? Okay. Give me some Valium or something, you can have it free. Just pull over now, okay? I ain't got all night."

"Look, let's just talk a minute. My name is Martin."

"Terrific. My name's Martina."

"Really?"

"Whatever. I ain't got no time for this."

"You did involve me in your life. You have to admit that. And now that I'm involved I'm responsible, and I can't leave you on a highway at 4:00 in the morning 'cause there's a lot of dangerous people out there, as you well know. And no matter how tough you talk you could get hurt. You're no older than seventeen, are you?"

"Are you some kind of census taker, or maybe you're one of the dangerous people yourself."

"Not at all. I'm a nice person, or I want to be."

"So what nice thing are you planning to do, Martin? Do you have a nice house you want to take me to?"

"Pretty nice, yeah. It's an apartment."

"So what do you want to do in this pretty nice apartment? You planning to slice up my bones into little bite-sized pieces?"

"What are you talking about? It's a place where you can stay tonight."

"Oh, yeah. Where is this place?"

"Santa Vista."

"And how'm I gonna get back, Martin? You wouldn't want me to ride on a stinking bus or have to hitchhike back to L.A., would you?"

"You can stay as long as you want. You don't have to go back to L.A."

"I get it. Steal the bitch. Then jump the bitch's bones. Then cook the bitch. Hey, Martin, I'll jump out of the fucking car now and take my chances with the traffic. I mean it. I'm in no mood."

"Calm down, will you? Look, you're obviously very upset. I'll get off at the first exit and we'll go to a motel or whatever. I'll pay for you to have your own room, give you the key. I'll stay in a different room. In the morning, I'll drive you back, if that's what you want. How's that sound?"

"Fine," she said dully. She seemed to have calmed down but he couldn't be sure. They rode the next twenty minutes in silence. When he turned off on the exit to Carpinteria, she asked a few questions about him and that made him feel good and increasingly sure he'd made a wise decision.

At the Carpinteria Motor Inn he did exactly as he said he would, charging the two different rooms on his Visa card. He handed her the key and she told him he was a real sweet guy. He said that he was three doors away and that in the morning he'd give her a ride either back to L.A. or to his apartment in Santa Vista.

"I hope you'll choose Santa Vista," he said.

She smiled and said maybe she would. Then she opened her door, and he waved good-bye and went to his room.

It was a standard motel room with a shower. He thought about taking one but decided he was too tired. He knew he would have no trouble sleeping, feeling he had already accomplished something by driving Martina to a safe place. He folded his shirt and pants on the chair in front of the desk, and got under the covers.

But fifteen minutes later there was a knock on his door.

"It's me—Martina. Can I come in?"

"Sure, just a second." He put his shirt on and opened the door. She looked away from him as she walked toward the window.

"I couldn't sleep. I kept thinking about the guy that went off on me."

"Would you like to stay here?"

She sat down on the side of the bed. "I don't want to do anything, okay? Just lie down for a while till I calm down, then I'm going back to my room. All right?"

"Sure, pick a side," Martin said, pointing to the bed. She lay down on the side nearest the door, and Martin, feeling he had won a little victory, made sure their bodies didn't touch as he lay down facing the window.

"It's weird to think how many creepy people there are, you know," she said suddenly. Martin thought of his parents and winced. "I know," he said, but to himself he was thinking that he only felt sorry for his parents now. He was feeling strong and more positive inside.

"Creep streets, every one of 'em filled with creeps . . . make cockroaches look like princes . . . make maggots look like kings. My father hit me, you know, when I was growing up and I came here and now this stranger, this black mother, beats on me . . . some progress, huh?"

"You can stay at my place in Santa Vista. You'll be safe there."

"Maybe I should. I mean what's L.A. got to offer me? So . . . what's it like in Santa Vista?"

Martin felt his heart beat. He described as accurately as he could the harbor and beach, the restaurants with the view of the mountains, and the shops on State Street.

"Sounds pretty amazing. But why'd you want me staying at your place? Don't you have no girlfriend?"

"No, there's no girlfriend. So why should I have that place all to myself when I can share it with someone who could use it, like you?"

"Gee, that's really nice, Marty. But I still have trouble believing you don't have at least one little girlfriend stashed away in Santa Vista."

"No, really."

"'Cause you're an attractive man. When you let me in I couldn't help noticing you got great legs."

Martin mumbled a thank you and felt himself blush, then realized she probably couldn't see him in the dark.

"Hey Marty, you use the shower here yet?"

"No, should I? Do I smell funny?"

"You smell real good. I mentioned it because it's a really fabulous shower. You can vary the water pressure, you know. Personally I like it really hard; it felt great on my body. Made it all tingly."

"I'll take one first thing in the morning."

"Between that shower and seeing your legs, I'm having trouble keeping my hands off you."

"You don't have to."

"Don't tempt me, but I think I ought to take things slow with you at first. See what things are like in Santa Vista."

"If you don't like it, I'll drive you back to L.A."

"Sounds real good, Marty," she said, leaning over and kissing him on the cheek. Martin smiled and squeezed her hand. "But let's sleep on it. I'm gonna go back to my room to sleep 'cause you're starting to excite me too much and I don't want to do something I'll regret later. But can I just lie here for a while before I go?"

"Of course," he said. He wanted to sleep himself and was still sure he'd have little trouble doing it. Positive things were definitely happening. He thought that she couldn't help but like the town and that she'd end up staying—that this could well be a turning point in both their lives, although they didn't know it now.

Martin fell asleep easily and dreamed he was lying in the midst of a group of large jagged rocks that the sea slapped against relentlessly. He was wearing a bathing suit and the sun felt good on his stomach, making him feel cared for, in a strange way, and remarkably satisfied.

A noise completely foreign to the dream he was having woke him up. Martina was by the chair where his pants were.

"What are you doing?" he said, although he knew that she was robbing him and a part of him had always known she would.

"Nothing. Getting some Kleenex."

He thought of simply letting her take the money but his sense of fairness wouldn't allow it. He turned on the bed light and she let out a short hollow scream, her face looking shocked in the sudden light like a Halloween mask. She had been stuffing his money into an opening in her stockings.

He stood up and Martina screamed again. "What you gonna do? You gonna kill me for taking some of your stinking creep money?"

She was trying to backpedal toward the door but tripped and fell to the floor.

"Come on and kill me Creep King. I fell, so here's your chance."

She stood up awkwardly and glared at him, half in rage, half in terror.

"I'm not gonna do anything," Martin said softly. "Take a hundred and leave the rest, okay?"

"The rich fucking creep saint has spoken! 'Take a hundred,' he says. You gotta always feel superior, right? You gotta always win. Here," she said, throwing two fifties at him and running out the door with two hundred dollars.

He didn't chase her. He didn't even pick up the money, just stared at the bills which looked like two dead lizards on the floor.

. . . .

He never knew how much time had passed before he went to the window. Nor did he have any idea what time it was when he lifted the blinds, only that it was mostly black out and that the light he did see came from stores or passing cars.

While he waited he went over everything that had happened between them, and all the words they had said to each other. In particular, he reviewed the last fight a number of times. He thought that if he had meant nothing to her and she just wanted his money, she wouldn't have bothered insulting him. He felt that he had touched something in her and that her anger was proof of it. What happened between them was therefore authentic in its own mysterious way.

He didn't know how long he stayed at the windows that night, either, only that he was never tempted to leave or even to sleep. The sky broke blue quickly, the sun shone out strong over the smog. He was surprised that a tear fell down his face, but let it fall. He kept looking up into the shining blue sky thinking that he had won something, that distorted and brief as it was he had had his first sip of love and so could remember everything that had happened with Martina and look at the sky and not feel weightless. That he, Martin, at twenty-two, had finally created a durable memory, and there was little chance now that it would ever leave him.

GHOST PARKS

His wife, Ellen, had yelled at him, then left to go to work at the museum, somehow implying that he, too, should work on Saturdays to better himself. She thought nothing of his current job, that was obvious. Selling disgusted her. It disgusted him, too, but he couldn't see any real difference between her job and his (wasn't she selling herself everyday to her bosses?), so why criticize? And why yell? She made him feel seven years old again, trembling with rage as if before his mother. Why did he put up with this? He felt he was getting so old now; he was already past thirty and he was still being yelled at by his wife. It was ridiculous, but there it was.

Andy paced in front of the picture window. Outside the sky was almost insanely bright. He looked down repeatedly at the elementary school playground where the basketball court was, but no one was on it. It was cold and he could hear the wind, but the court looked good in the strong sunlight.

There was a line, Andy thought, as clear as the foul line on a basketball court, and she had crossed it. Certainly, there were a number of ways you could cross the line—he'd thought for some time that she would cross it with a single outrageous act like sleeping with her boss. He still thought she'd probably done that, but he couldn't prove it. Instead she'd crossed it with her yelling and the abusive things she said. It was not any single thing she said, but rather the number of times she said them, the number of times she yelled at him until she yelled herself right across that line.

He stopped pacing, looked out the window again, and realized that it was over—that much was certain. There was something pure about knowing this, something as pure as the sky. Still he felt nervous, as if uncomfortable in his own skin, and decided that despite the weather, he'd go outside and shoot some baskets, by himself if necessary.

It was more windy than he expected, and unusually cold that morning even for December, but he was still glad to be outdoors. His first thought was to go to Taney Park five blocks away on Pine Street, but then he remembered that the new Park Commissioner had taken the rims off the backboards to keep blacks away. Just like that, one hundred people disappeared. Some of the white players in the neighborhood even complained, but it came to nothing. Now the single basket on the elementary school playground three blocks from his apartment was the only place left to shoot in Center City. Philadelphia was getting more stupid every day, he thought, destroying its own playgrounds for no reason. This basket, which he was now forced to use, was old with a large gray wooden backboard and a slightly over-sized rim so that you could never even be sure you deserved the shot you made. Most of the time Andy didn't let that bother him, but this morning it bothered him a lot. Moreover, after his first basket he missed his next six shots. It was the wind, it was the sun in his eyes, but most of all he was still stunned by his latest fight with Ellen and the realization that she had begun to hate him, and perhaps had hated him for some time.

That he hated her was completely different. He was sure she didn't know, so as long as he kept it a secret it didn't hurt anyone. Besides, his was not a cold or pure hatred—it had been balanced by memories of happier times with her and by the desire he still felt. He often thought of it as a close and vastly complicated basketball game—a game of streaks. When she got angry or wouldn't sleep with him the Hate Team surged ahead, but if she were nice even for ten or fifteen minutes, the other team would rally. But always it was a game he was officiating, and if it got too lopsided one way or the other he could end it and make it disappear.

This morning while she yelled at him he had seen something in her face that was undeniable. She wasn't playing any secret game; she wasn't ambivalent. She simply hated him and it shocked him, though he knew things had been going badly for some time. She was bitterly disappointed in their marriage and was probably sleeping with someone or soon would. She would never want him again as she once had—his sex life with her was lost. His own complicated game was now over as well. The look in her eyes had ended it in an instant. That look made her cross the line even more than her yelling, he realized. He hated her totally now and only hoped she would leave him soon or else let him go. If she wouldn't, if she were afraid of having to pay alimony or else was insane enough to expect some from him (for he had some money from his parents), he'd do something if he had to, anything to be rid of her.

Finally, he made a hook shot. Andy turned instinctively to see if anyone was watching, and saw a black man coming toward him, wrapped in a cheap green cloth coat that reminded him of the army coat he used to wear in college in the sixties. The man had a thin beard which circled his face and gave him a look of sternness and conviction. Andy thought they were about the same age, that he was maybe an inch or two taller, though it was hard to tell because the man was walking hunched over a little with both arms folded against the cold.

Finally, Andy turned to him. "Wanna shoot?"

The man unfolded his arms and opened his hands to catch the ball. For a few minutes they shot in silence. Andy immediately considered himself a better player and hoped there'd be no challenge for a one-on-one. He hated such situations where he had to determine how hard he should try so that the game could be close, and no one would be too hurt or angry. He'd been the starting off-guard on his high school team and generally was one of the best players on any given day at a playground, though of course he'd slowed up a little in the last few years.

"Damn! Can't get one to go down," the man said.

"The wind's brutal. You gotta play the wind today."

They shot another two minutes without speaking. Andy thought about Ellen and began missing his shots again. When the man hit a couple of jumpers, Andy said, "All right!" with sportscaster enthusiasm.

The man walked over to him carrying the ball and extending his free hand. "My name's Graham."

"I'm Andy." They shook hands and Andy asked if he lived nearby.

Graham said no and Andy immediately regretted his question because Graham looked like he was probably homeless. His chinos were badly torn and his shoes looked like strips of bacon. Ellen had upset him so much he couldn't think right any more.

"Hey, man, I want to show you something."

Graham reached inside the pocket of his coat, which came down to his knees, and pulled out a wallet. "See this? I used to be in a group, man. You know music?"

"Sure, some."

"Here's a picture of my group. We was called 'The Thunderballs.'"

Andy nodded. He had never heard of them. He saw a picture of four black men in tuxedos smiling in front of some palm trees and asked what Graham did in the group.

"Sang, played keyboards, sometimes sang lead. We travelled all over when things was good. Then we hit a down time in L.A. See this dude? Recognize him? That's Quincy Jones."

"Sure." It was a colored Polaroid—all the pictures were—of Graham standing next to Jones in a club. Andy found himself checking for inauthentic details, in spite of himself. Graham showed him similar pictures of himself and Whitney Houston, his group hovering around Danny DeVito (of all people), his group sitting at a table with Luther Vandross, and then one of himself and a smiling Cher.

"Amazing," Andy said, in part to make Graham feel good, in part because he was kind of amazed to see a picture of this street person in such friendly proximity to Cher, who had long been one of his fantasy women.

"Yeah, things were cool for awhile."

"What happened?"

"Give me the rock, man; I've got to stay warm."

Graham hit a jump shot and Andy applauded. He thought that he had to do this to keep Graham talking.

"Income tax problems is what happened. I didn't do it. Just trusted the wrong people. Shoulda stayed with the brothers, I guess. Done three years for it, I know that."

"Prison?"

"Three-and-a-half years' time. Just out a few weeks ago."

"How come you're in Philly?"

"Long story, man. I'm trying to get down to Florida. Got a wife and kid in Jacksonville," Graham sighed. "Yeah, I really miss 'em."

Andy stopped himself from asking Graham why he didn't go to Jacksonville. It was obvious he had no money.

"You gotta old lady?" Graham said with a little smile that showed a chipped front tooth.

"Yeah, but I'm trying to get away from her. Can't stand her anymore. She yells at me all the time."

"That's cold."

"Yeah, it shouldn't happen, should it?"

Graham shook his head. "Come on, check me, man" Graham said. He began dribbling with rapid, low bounces toward the imaginary key.

"Remember Earl the Pearl? Watch this." Graham tried a spin move, but his shot only nicked a side of the rim. Then he insisted on going through the routine three more times until he finally made a basket—Andy all the while playing only token defense. After his basket Graham said, "See that, the Pearl is back. Now I'll turn into Clyde Frazier and check you. You old enough to remember those dudes, ain't you? How old are you?"

"Too old to keep guarding you. You're wearing me out." He still wanted to avoid a game, and besides he'd gotten an idea that was still so vague he didn't know if it was an idea or a dream, but to find out he knew he needed to talk some more to Graham. Andy took a jump shot, missed, got his own rebound and passed the ball to Graham.

"Let's just shoot, O.K.?"

Graham rubbed the ball and smiled. "Long as I get to shoot the rock, I'm happy. Long as you have a rock, you're never alone, right man?"

"Right," Andy said, but he hardly heard him. He was thinking about his idea again and for the next five minutes, while they shot, he tried furiously to remember bank statements and deeds and insurance policies. When he was unable to visualize each document he felt that it might no longer exist, and he'd start to panic. Then he'd turn his back and dribble the ball hard on the concrete with his eyes closed until he found he could see the lease or the last bank statement, could make them exist again through concentration. He turned to Graham. "Where are you staying now?"

Graham smiled ironically and shrugged. "No place particular, man. I'm trying to get enough together for a room but they want all this security shit, first two months, then the last month . . . Maybe they're insecure or something," he laughed. "Course you can't get a job if you don't have an address." He swore and spat with disgust, the wind barely letting the spit leave him.

"Sounds rough. I'm sorry."

"I don't know what they expect when they let you out. They don't give you nothing . . . you can't get a job, that's almost impossible. I'm trying to be good. I'm trying not to slip up and do something wrong, but they're not making it easy. Every day I'm tempted 'cause I got to eat, you know? Yeah, I'm tempted every day."

Andy looked at Graham closely. His big dark eyes looked angry, and for a moment Andy was frightened.

"You could stay with me for a while, if it wasn't for my wife. She wouldn't go for it. She doesn't care about helping people. She's one of these unconscious racists, if you know what I mean. She doesn't know herself well enough to even understand it, but she is."

"I hear you."

"But look, I can give you a few bucks so you can eat something today."

"Thank you, man."

"I'll have to get it in my apartment, if you don't mind walking me there."

"That's no problem."

They took their last shots, each waiting till the other made a basket, then left the playground, walking up Chestnut Street. Andy lived in a high-rise filled with what he considered yuppie creeps and future yuppie creeps (University of Pennsylvania business students). It was his wife's idea to move there. He'd wanted to stay in West Philly where they'd lived near Clark Park, a playground where there were always lots of games and where he'd earned something of a reputation. But after Ellen's promotion, she'd insisted on moving. She became impossible on the subject so quickly he couldn't muster a defense. She was hot to live at a semistatus address, and also, Andy thought, hot to get away from black people. Their new building fulfilled both her wishes. Except for the doorman and maintenance men, who were all black, and a prostitute accompanying a blushing business student, he'd never seen a black person *inside* the building. Just another example of apartheid Philadelphia-style, he thought. That Ellen loved the building convinced him she was a racist and made him hate her all the more. As they climbed the steps to his building, he wondered if he should introduce Graham to James, the somewhat supercilious doorman now on duty, but decided to say nothing. So a poor black man in shabby clothes was in the building; let the building make an issue of it. He knew the building wouldn't, that the building would back down.

When they walked into the lobby, James looked at Graham with slightly raised eyebrows, but as soon as Andy looked at him, James buzzed them both in. On the elevator the presence of Margaret, the legal secretary who lived on the same floor, temporarily inhibited them, but as soon as they began walking down the hallway, they started talking again.

"You got a nice building, man."

"The accommodations are nice, but the people are a different story."

Andy turned the key, and they walked into his apartment. "Make yourself at home, sit down if you can find someplace where there isn't a plant or tree growing. My wife likes to pretend she lives in the jungle—a high rise in the jungle, I guess. But no natives, just her and the trees."

Graham sat in a brown leather chair and laughed. "Reminds me of my time in California."

"Wanna beer?" Andy asked as he opened the refrigerator.

"Sure."

Andy took out two cans of Heineken. "I can't find a clean glass. Is the can O.K.?"

"Sure, man. Can's great."

He handed Graham the Heineken and sat down in a green La-Z-Boy opposite him. To their left a large picture window overlooked Center City. Periodically they looked out the window while they drank and talked.

"That the playground where we was?" Graham said, pointing at the window and then momentarily turning toward Andy. Andy nodded.

"Do you check it out to see who's there before you go down? Is that what you do?"

"Sometimes," Andy said, while Graham laughed.

"You got a real setup man. Yes sir, a real setup."

Andy didn't say anything. He didn't want to begin talking until they'd both had a second beer or something stronger. He was trying to remember where he had hidden his pot (his smoking was another thing Ellen and he fought about), thinking the pot might be what he needed to implement his idea. Meanwhile, Graham was talking about his salad days in California.

"When I was in Santa Monica I was three minutes from the beach. That's three minutes if I ran, and I used to run there at first, just to see how fast I could get there. That was beautiful, man. The waves and the sun."

"What was your place like?"

"Two-room apartment we were renting. Got a little crowded 'cause one of the guys in the group was staying there too."

He felt a flash of jealousy which he tried to stop by focusing on Graham's present condition. Graham was looking at him quizzically.

"Course, even though I could get to the beach in three minutes, I couldn't see it from my window, man. You're three minutes from the park and you can see it too. That's a setup. Yes sir, you're in a real classy building."

"I didn't want to come here. I liked where I was before better, but my wife made me move. She wanted a big deal address."

"Where were you before?"

"In West Philly, in a regular apartment. I was near a park too. I couldn't see it from my window, but there were games there all the time with all kinds of people. I don't have anyone to talk to here. Everyone here is the same, if you know what I mean."

"I hear you."

Andy felt odd, as if he were starting to vibrate inside, and took a breath to steady himself.

"I'm getting another brew," he announced.

"Sure, man. We gonna drink the blues away." Graham laughed and Andy laughed too, before stopping himself in the kitchen. He would get nowhere acting like this; he would lose track of his idea. He decided he should change the mood, so when he returned with the beers he asked Graham about his wife and child.

They were in L.A. with him when he was arrested and had gone back to Jacksonville to stay with her relatives, Graham explained. His son, Tommy, was four-and-a-half years old, and for three of those years Graham hadn't seen him. Andy looked at the pain on Graham's face and felt nervous.

"You and your wife have any children?" Graham said.

"Well, there's the two of us," he said, and Graham laughed.

"See my wife doesn't want to have any children. There's not much happening in our bed these days. She thinks she's so successful now that she doesn't have to deal with the likes of me. Want some of this?" he said, holding out a joint and lighter he'd found next to the steak knives in the kitchen.

Graham gave him a funny look. "With my empty stomach, this gonna go right to my head." But he took the joint, inhaled deeply a couple of times, and passed it back to Andy.

"Like I said before, I can give you about ten bucks or so. Wish I could give you more, but that's all I got on me. My wife makes most of the money, and she doesn't share. She hides all her cash, too." He took a hit, passed it back to Graham, then waited until Graham smoked some more.

"Your woman ever cold to you? I mean one or two times they all say no."

"Yeah, one or two times a week, you mean," Graham said laughing.

"Yeah, really," Andy said, forcing himself to laugh. He waited until Graham stopped laughing, which seemed to take a long time, then said, "No, I mean has she ever shut you down for a long period of time?"

"A long time?" Graham asked.

"Yeah."

"Course that's one of those relative terms. 'Cause sometimes a week's a long time and sometimes a day is. Every damn day I spent in jail was long to me."

"I was thinking more like a month than a week."

"No man, that never happened to me 'cept in jail."

"I hate it when they use their pussies as a weapon to shut you down."

"Hey, better they should shut you down than chop you down, right? Like that Lorena Bobbitt did to her husband while he was sleeping. John Bobbitt was his name, wasn't it? Then she drove off and threw it away like an old useless bone. Cold, man."

"Yeah, she got off with nothing man, nothing but a little counseling, as I recall. Hell, she probably enjoyed whining about herself and having someone there who had to listen. That was probably pleasure for her. I know my wife would rather complain than anything."

Andy inhaled on the last of the joint then said, "What did you say you were arrested for?"

"I told you, man, income tax problems. My manager did it. I trusted the wrong dude, that's all."

"That's a lot of time for income taxes."

"Hey, you ever notice life ain't always fair?"

"Right," Andy said, nodding. "Must have been tough in jail. Was there a lot of violent stuff in there?"

"What you think? Wasn't no tea party. You got to be alert, you got to take care of yourself. That's why I can do it now on the streets. I learned how to survive in there."

"But you said you aren't getting into any fights now."

"No. I'm not fighting anyone 'less they fight me first. I told you that. What you think? I tell you one thing on the playground and another up here?"

Andy made a conciliatory gesture with his hands. "Not at all. I'm just trying to understand. 'Cause you said you were tempted."

"Sure, I'm tempted."

"That's interesting 'cause there are probably other people who are tempted too, who might pay you a lot of money to do something for them."

"You mean, pay me to pull some job for them?"

Andy finished the joint and tried to make eye contact with Graham.

"It could be that or something that might be worth a lot more money to you."

"Like what?"

"Say there was a man who really hated someone he was living with.

Say this man had been stepped on and humiliated by this person and felt he'd come to the end of the line." He felt his hand shake but kept on. "Now he might not be a man who looks like he has money, but he might really have some money plus be absolutely sure of getting some more so he could put, say, ten thousand bucks in your pocket. Let's also say that he already has an excellent plan worked out, and he's only looking for someone like you to put the plan in motion so he can put a stop to the cruelty of this terrible person he happens to live with."

Graham leaned forward in his chair. "Am I reading you right? You serious?"

"Could be, Graham. You might be."

"Well, that person wouldn't be looking for me 'cause I wouldn't be doing nothing like that. I draw the line, see. And on one side of the line is money and property, and on the other side is people, even racist pigs—unconscious or otherwise. They're still on that side of the line."

Graham looked directly at him, and a terrible fear swept though Andy.

"That's a very good answer," Andy said. "That's a really impressive answer."

"There's lots of temptation out there, but that ain't one of them. Never be one either. I'm a father, you know. You can't bring one person into the world and take another out. I'll be going now."

Both men got up from their chairs, and Andy mumbled something about how strong Graham's character was. Then he took fifteen dollars from his pocket and thrust it into Graham's hands, worrying that Graham might realize that he'd had money in his pants all along, but not wanting to lie about it either.

Graham said, "Thanks," and put the money in his coat. He had pulled his coat tightly around himself and was heading toward the door.

Andy rushed up behind him and began asking if maybe they could meet to play ball again. He picked up the basketball from in front of the door and followed Graham out into the hallway, but Graham was already standing by the elevator. "Hey," he said, passing the ball to him, "take it. It's yours."

Graham looked down at the ball he had caught, running his fingers over it for a few seconds as if he were combing an animal's fur before he passed it back to Andy. "You need it more than I do," he said. Then the elevator came and Graham left.

In his apartment Andy paced in front of his picture window thinking that Graham saw right through him, which was why he wouldn't take the ball or even say good-bye. But what would Graham do? Would he go to the police, or try to warn Ellen some way, maybe leave a message for her with the doorman?

He ran into the bedroom and, after searching the room quickly, found Ellen's Ativan in the bathroom cabinet. He took a pill and returned to the living room, letting his head fill with a different voice that the mere taking of the Ativan seemed to have set in motion.

He thought, I've been smoking, which is making everything seem worse. The bottom line is it's his word against mine (and I never even, technically, said anything), plus he's a homeless ex-con who's high. Besides, he took the money so he can eat—he just wants to eat. He doesn't want any new trouble; that'd be the last thing he wants.

He sat down in the brown leather chair and his anxiety began to give way to an immense sadness. He started running his fingers over the leaves of a jade plant. How had he come to this point? He could still vividly remember the time when they loved each other. What had happened to those people? It was like time just took them away and replaced them with two angry ghosts. At any rate, he now knew he wouldn't have gone through with it. It was only a temporary rage he was in and now it was over. When Graham spoke of drawing the line, he'd felt strangely moved. He stopped stroking the plant and stood up to see if Graham might be back on the playground or else walking on the street, but all he could see were buildings and the blinding blue sky. It was too cold to be out walking, much too cold.

A few hours later, he fell asleep in the bedroom. When he heard the door open he woke up instantly, but instinctively stayed still.

"Christ, what a day," Ellen was muttering, either to herself or to him, he couldn't tell which. He could hear her undressing, making more noises of exasperation in the room. Be nice, he warned himself. Things can be made better just by being nice. But he was afraid that if he talked she'd find out he'd been high and pick another fight. Tomorrow he'd be nice first thing, but for now it was best to say nothing and just vanish. So he closed his eyes, pretending to be asleep, but the uncomfortable feeling in his skin returned, and for a moment, he thought again of hiring someone else for the job Graham wouldn't do. His head ached, too, but he'd get no sympathy talking about that to Ellen, so he just kept his eyes closed and soon rolled over to make room for her in their bed.

MERCURY

There was a party in TriBeCa, what Larry thought would be the same group of writers his age or older complaining and consoling each other. The party's host, Aaron Reisman, once had a brief flurry of success with his metafictionist stories, but that had all ended years ago. In fact, Aaron had already, in his own words, "surrendered" to his "bad karma" and now wrote only for an hour or two every other weekend. His one enduring piece of good fortune was the loft he'd bought cheap in the late '70s, which, of course, had now sky-rocketed in value. Every year, shortly before Christmas, he'd have a party in his loft for the writers and sympathizers in his circle who all brought wine or whiskey (Aaron somehow constructed the dip), and each year the humor got a little more desperate and bitter.

Until the last minute, Larry thought that this year he'd skip the party. He was in a writing slump, badly stalled on a novel he'd been working on since his book of stories had been published three years ago. Moreover, he was out of fulltime work now, wholly reliant on substitute teaching to make money. Under the circumstances, with all that was on his mind, how could he stand to go to Aaron's party? Still, there was one reason to consider going. He'd heard a rumor that Kenneth Alters would be there. Initially he'd dismissed it as an attempt of Aaron's to ensure a good crowd or maybe a fantasy of one of the guests. Why would a young, glamorous writer/celebrity like Kenneth Alters attend such a scruffy affair? Yet, such things did happen in New York and he couldn't discount it. The more he thought about meeting Alters, perhaps even being able to befriend him and all that might mean, the harder it got to stay home. Finally, he drank a glass of vodka and soda water, then selected a pair of jeans and a purple wool sweater, trying not to look overly concerned about his clothes but not wholly unattractive either. Then, before he'd gotten halfway to the elevator, he went back to his apartment to get a copy of his book of stories, and his knife. He'd been mugged by three teenagers a few months ago and without telling anyone, had bought a large pocket knife which he generally took with him now whenever he went out at night.

There were dark clouds outside and he nearly ran from the corner liquor store (where he bought a bottle of gin for the party) to the train stop. On the train to TriBeCa he spent the whole trip thinking about Kenneth Alters' sudden and stunning success.

An elevator led directly to Aaron's loft on the fourth floor where Larry was greeted by the familiar scene of men mostly on the edge of middle age in their de rigeur minimalist dress of jeans and tee shirts, men who still looked puzzled as to why their stomachs were sticking out and their hair lines receding, holding their drinks while they talked to each other or to the mostly younger women they were with. But the loud laughter and quasi-hysterical talk that usually filled the air was strangely muted. Larry thought that it was like a theater shortly before the lights dimmed. The glances were mostly directed toward the punch bowl in the right side center of the loft where Kenneth Alters, looking infuriatingly as good as his photographs, was standing alone, cool and self-contained in a gray suit and baby-blue tie.

Immediately Larry went to the bar, about twenty feet behind Alters, and fixed himself a vodka tonic, leaving his bottle of gin on an adjacent table. When he looked up again, Alters was still standing alone. In a bizarre (yet somehow predictable) gesture of collective insecurity or perverse pride the other guests were pretending not to pay any attention to Alters, although, periodically, everyone in the room was actually looking at him. What provincial idiots they are, Larry thought. Someone a little famous comes to their party, and immediately he paralyzes the room. He drank his vodka quickly, deciding that the less he thought about what to say to Alters, the better. He would simply tell him that he admired his work (he had only allowed himself to read a single story of Alters', which he'd considered more precious than precocious) and then at some point tell him about his own book, hopefully giving him the paperback copy he'd brought. It was imagining all the consequences (that never happened anyway) and giving time for anxieties to multiply that intimidated people.

When Larry finished his drink he began walking directly toward Alters, then seeing that he was talking with Aaron, he went to get another vodka from the bar. With his new drink in hand he looked out at the rest of the loft and soon noticed an attractive brunette, a poet he'd spoken to for a few minutes at a couple of downtown parties. For some reason, probably because of his fixation with his former lover Debby, he'd never called her and couldn't even remember her name. Was it Jama, Janette, Janine? Anyway, it was "J" something, so he thought of her as Lady J. She was talking to Morty, a forty-something writer who dressed like a hippie and wrote simple-minded parable-like stories—a third-rate Brautigan. Lady J, wearing a very nicely cut black dress, looked like she was humoring Morty. Larry began to move toward her but before he could make any meaningful progress he was stopped by a less attractive woman, a redhead with darting, almost comically intense green eyes.

Gesturing slightly with her head, she said, "Is that who I think it is?"

"That's Kenneth Alters, himself."

She looked perplexed and astonished. She was overly dressed, Larry thought, and was wearing too much makeup and jewelry.

"Wasn't he on the cover of *People* last week?"

"He wasn't on the cover, but they did a story on him," Larry said.

"Yeah, that's right. It was about this three-picture movie deal he signed. God, can you imagine being that successful at his age and that rich, if you can believe the story."

"Normally, I don't read those kind of magazines but since I'm a writer myself, I was curious to see what they'd say. It's so rare that they do an article about a writer."

"You write novels, too?"

"Yes, and short stories."

"Do I know your name?"

"Larry James."

Larry watched her studying him skeptically for a few seconds as if he might be lying about being a writer. The thought made him bristle and he finished his second drink. She looked like a poor man's Lucille Ball anyway, he thought.

"So have you met Alters yet?"

"No, I haven't."

"Oh," she said with what Larry thought was obvious disappointment. "I was going to ask you to introduce me, but what the hell, he's just a person. I can introduce myself. After I've had a couple of drinks," she said, laughing loudly. Larry tried to supress his anger while he waited for her laughter to subside, then excused himself, still keeping his eyes on Alters who was giving Aaron a lot of time.

He went to the bar and fixed himself a new vodka tonic. It was strange to think that just three years ago Alters was completely unknown. That's when his first book of stories had gotten both extraordinary reviews and sales. A host of articles with pictures of the young, golden-haired writer began appearing everywhere as if he were a movie star. Of course, Alters' youth (he was only twenty-five, ten years younger than Larry) was used to help promote him as a phenomenon. That and the brilliant way Alters himself marketed his California friendliness. Surprisingly, his antisnobbism was seen, even by cynical New Yorkers, not as disingenuous but as refreshing. At the time Larry reassured himself that his own first collection, published the same year, had also gotten some very good, thoughtful reviews, though his small press publisher could hardly compete with Alters' major New York house in getting anything like the amount of attention Alters got. Still he could at least consider himself a part of the same general literary universe. But when Alters' novel, published just last year, eclipsed the success of his first book and became a bestseller, everything changed. Now at twenty-eight, Alters really did inhabit a different literary and social world. He'd been on late-night talk shows, there were articles speculating that he might act in one of the movies that he was writing, and in an interview with the *Times* he expressed an interest in directing. Could one doubt it would happen? When he moved to New York and bought a loft in SoHo, *New York Magazine* wrote about it. Columbia University immediately signed him to teach one hour a week for who knows how much money, and seemingly every university or writers' series in the city wanted him to read or lecture—offers that Alters kept accepting. To top it off, despite his bestseller, Alters had actually increased his involvement in *Mercury,* the young literary magazine of which he'd been West Coast editor and which had also enjoyed a quick rise in status. It was as if he couldn't bear to let go of anything in his impeccable resume, and now that he'd moved to New York, where the magazine was published, he'd become associate editor, and the main fiction editor as well.

Larry finished his drink and noticed that Alters was finally alone, but Aaron had spotted Larry and was smiling broadly as if he wanted a witness to congratulate him on his social coup.

"Glad you came, Larry," Aaron said as they shook hands.

"How could I miss this," he said, gesturing toward Alters, who was still alone.

"How's it going these days? Nobody ever sees you anymore."

"I need a job for one thing. Substitute teaching is all I've got now."

"I'll definitely let you know if I hear of anything. How's Debby? Are you two together by any chance?"

Larry looked away for a moment. "No, we're not. So how's Kenneth Alters?"

"Very nice."

"I guess I'll pay him my humble respects now."

"By all means, you'll enjoy him."

"Then I'll talk to you later," he said, patting Aaron on the shoulder.

"Good luck," Aaron said, smiling even more broadly than before.

Alters, whose wavy blonde hair reached to the tops of his shoulders, looked to be consulting his watch. Was he planning an early exit, already regretting that he'd attended this nebulous event?

"Excuse me, I'm Larry James," he said, shaking Alters' hand. "Like everyone else, I admire your work a great deal and I'm glad you've come to New York."

"Thank you, Larry," he said with his by now famous smile, long lashes shading twinkling eyes.

"It must be a very exciting time for you."

"It's been busy more than anything. I've certainly spent more time with agents, lawyers, and interior decorators than I've ever wanted to."

"You've become an event."

Alters laughed and took a sip from a drink that Larry hadn't noticed. "I understand that you're also becoming more involved with *Mercury.*"

"That's true, too."

"The magazine is really hot these days. It keeps getting terrific publicity."

"I hope I don't jinx it."

"I don't think that there's much chance of that. You're the main reason it's so successful."

Alters looked at him more seriously for a moment. "I don't think so, but thanks again. Are you a writer by any chance?"

"Yes, I am. I published a first collection of stories with a small press the same year you published your first book. And I'm working on a novel."

"What's the name of your book?"

Larry looked down at the floor for a second. *"Rights of the Moon . . . and Other Stories,"* he said spelling out the word "Rights." "It was done by a small press and . . ."

Alters knit his eyebrows for a moment.

"I'm sorry I don't know it, but I'll try to get a copy."

"It's a pretty weird title but . . ."

"Don't apologize. I like it. It sounds different from so many other collections that come out these days." Alters turned to the vodka punch bowl. "Want a drink?" he said. "It's not bad stuff."

Larry thanked him and took a new drink, thinking that Alters was being pretty decent—though he didn't like the words "Don't apologize." Christ, Alters was almost young enough to be his student, yet there he was being subtly patronizing. He took a big sip of punch and asked Alters what he would be doing now at *Mercury.*

"Reading lots of fiction."

"I wonder why you feel the need . . ." And then, seeing Alters' face tighten, Larry quickly added, "Or have the time when your own writing is so successful."

"It's something I've always cared about and enjoyed doing. I've always been involved in literary magazines. At least since high school. Maybe it's my kind of security blanket."

"And you still need it, successful as you are?" Larry said, trying to control the edge in his voice.

"You can never have too much security, can you?"

"So you're going to be the main fiction editor, then?"

"That's what they tell me."

"Any changes you plan to make? Anything in particular you're looking for?"

"Umm . . . I guess, as the cliché says, every editor likes to make discoveries."

"Oh. So you plan to publish fewer famous people then?"

The tightness reappeared in Alters' eyes.

"I mean, in the past *Mercury* has published a lot of famous people, and now you'll be looking for unknowns?"

"The famous people will not entirely disappear, but we will be looking to showcase more unknown talent."

"Does unknown mean young?"

"I'm not sure I follow you."

"Take me for instance. I was young once and unknown and now, as you can see, I've gotten older and my hair's thinning and so forth. I'm sure I've got at least ten years on you, but I did publish this one book in a small edition and it did get some good reviews, some of them as good as the reviews you got, even, and some of the stories in this book had been published in pretty good literary magazines, too. So do I qualify as an unknown or am I just a little too old to qualify and so fall somewhere between the cracks?"

He was aware that he was rambling, that something unpleasantly aggressive was happening when he spoke, but he couldn't seem to stop it.

"I'd be interested in seeing anything that's good published in *Mercury*."

This seemed unsatisfactorily evasive and Larry felt stung. Perhaps he should force the issue and give him the copy of his book now.

"Well, assuming you mean it, maybe I'll take you at your word and send something your way."

"You seem skeptical."

"Skeptical?"

"And a little cynical."

"Like I say, I've been around awhile and I've seen this kind of thing."

"What thing is this?"

"Some new young person comes along who gets sensational press, signs a big book deal and then figures it's smart to do something 'altruistic,' fears there might be some kind of backlash of resentment otherwise and so gets nominally involved in a project that's supposed to help young writers. Like Norman Mailer starting the *Village Voice*. It happens all the time."

"Well, I'm not 'some young person.' I'm a real person just like you are and I do care about writing by young people and older people, but I don't think I like the way this conversation's going."

"What's wrong with the conversation?"

"It seems tense and a little angry and also aimed at making me acknowledge some dark crime of hideous self-interest. Outside of that, nothing."

"Look, I'm just a hard-working writer trying to get somewhere and not succeeding very well," Larry said, looking slightly to the left of Alters while he spoke. "I don't even have a job or a girlfriend and I meet someone like you, which doesn't happen very often, and I hear you talk about helping unknowns and I wonder how you could know at your age what it means to be unknown, to struggle year after year in bad living conditions. I mean a bug-infested, heat-saturated apartment like I live in where you can hear your neighbor's answering machine, hear his toilet flush 'cause the walls are so thin, and meanwhile people are selling crack in my neighborhood and on any given night I can get mugged like I was two months ago so that now when I go out I have to carry a knife."

"Do I need to know all of this to be the fiction editor of a literary magazine?"

"I just wonder, if you want to help young writers so much why don't you finance a magazine instead and let some talented lesser-known writers edit it."

"Like you?"

"No, not at all. Though I would know certain things about how to deal with unknown writers, especially the older ones who've been doing good work for a long time. What they've been through . . . and how to treat them. But, what I'm really wondering about is, if the world's given somebody everything right away, how can they judge others?"

"You do a fair amount of judging yourself, as far as I can see. Excuse me," Alters said, turning away.

"Don't blow me off like I'm a fly, like I don't exist. Why don't you stay and talk?"

But Alters had already left him and was surrounded by a semi-circle of people, some of whom were giving Larry funny looks. How loud had he been talking? How many people had heard him practically begging Alters to talk to him? The loft had snapped back into view, and he saw again the grotesque ballet of the guests as they assumed their strategic positions around Alters like so many little birds along the shoreline waiting, small and stupid and squawking, for something they hoped the next wave would deliver.

Larry turned back to the punch bowl and poured himself another drink, keeping his back to them. He finished the drink in four bitter swallows, then fixed himself another and drank it only a little more slowly.

Walking a few steps away from the people around Alters he closed his eyes. What had happened to him, why was he shaking in anger? It was as if he'd always felt this way, but that couldn't be true. He knew he was happy the day his book was accepted, but that was followed by so many days of anxiety trying to help market it and get it reviewed that he'd nearly sunk under the weight of it. No, the kind of happiness he was trying to remember was all bound up with women, especially Debby, but that was too painful to think about now. Suddenly he turned around— his eyes focusing immediately on Alters who was talking to Lady J., the brunette poet he'd fantasized about going out with. She was smiling almost as wide as Alters was, eating up his words as if listening to him were a kind of sex act that gave her ultimate gratification.

When he first started talking to Alters he'd figured he had an inch on him and simply by being older was probably more muscular, though with the loose clothes Alters wore, it was hard to tell what kind of body he had. Now as he walked toward him, he knew he was taller and bigger than Alters.

"Why did you walk away from me? Why did you insult me?" he said loudly, forcing Alters' conversation with Lady J to stop. He kept his eyes on Alters, who looked startled, profoundly disrupted, in fact. Lady J's mouth was open, and she, too, looked deeply confused.

"It's you who insulted me. Why don't you just leave me alone?"

"I want to know why you won't finish what we were talking about, man to man." Some more people had stopped talking and had begun gathering around them, including the overdressed redhead with the glaring green eyes.

"There isn't anything more I want to say to you."

"But you insulted me, and then . . ."

"Look, I don't want to spend any more time with you, that's all."

A worried-looking Aaron appeared in front of him.

"Come on Larry, stop it. You've had too much to drink. You're drunk."

He'd put an arm around his shoulder, but Larry threw it off. He remembered his knife then, felt it folded in his jacket pocket, thought he could feel it pressing, cold and heavy, against his flesh. Then he stepped forward and pushed Alters' shoulders. "You condescending little bitch."

Alters went back a couple of steps and the guests gasped. When Alters came back he threw a punch which grazed Aaron, who'd stepped between them again, in the neck. Aaron let out a yowl of pain but managed to grab Larry in a bear hug.

"You jealous jerk, are you out of your mind?" Alters said, teeth flashing.

"Come outside and fight me," Larry said in a voice he hadn't used since his playground fights twenty-five years ago.

"Please, Larry, stop it," Aaron said. Larry saw fear in Aaron's eyes and let himself be led away, a few feet at a time, while Aaron kept saying softly, pleadingly, "Just go home and rest Larry; you're drunk, go home and rest."

At the elevator door Larry turned and pointed at Alters but Alters had turned his back to him. Before he could yell again Aaron said "Please," his sad middle-aged brown eyes looking desperate. "Get in the elevator. Go home and you'll feel better."

Larry took a deep breath.

"I'm sorry for this," he said. "Really sorry."

"Just go home. Call me tomorrow if you want," Aaron added, before the elevator doors closed.

....

"Are you all right?" she said, an unintentional parody of concern on her face.

Alters looked around in an exaggerated manner at himself to try to make her laugh, then said, "As far as I know."

"Why did that maniac attack you?" she said, brushing a few recalcitrant strands of dark hair from her forehead, then rearranging her dress to make her breasts more prominent. Alters simply shook his head while she introduced herself as Janice.

"I'm Kenneth Alters," he said, shaking her hand.

"Of course, everyone knows who you are."

"As for my assailant, I have no idea. I was going to ask you. Is he a maniac or maybe he just drank too much and is angry at some image he's projected onto me."

"I've seen him at parties before. He tried to hit on me once but he didn't get anywhere," she said, trying to align her eyes with his.

"Well, nobody's punches landed though I'm afraid one of mine hit . . ." He paused, unsure if the host's name was Arthur, Arnold, or Aaron. ". . . the man who organized the party."

"Yes, wasn't that awful, I mean, awfully bad luck? But I'm sure he's all right."

"Oh, of course, I'm hardly Mike Tyson."

"In fact, here he is now."

Rather than guess from the trinity of names, Alters stepped forward and shook Aaron's hand. "Sorry that you caught my right hook. Obviously it wasn't meant for you."

Aaron, uncertain if Alters meant to be funny, was temporarily paralyzed between a laugh and an apology.

"I'm sorry that all this happened to you—when we all feel so lucky that you came here."

Alters winced and tuned out the remains of Aaron's tribute. He waited for an appropriate moment to lighten things up, but before he could a number of people began introducing themselves to him and shaking his hand. It was going to take a lot longer than he thought to get out of here.

The people who talked to him all exaggerated his virtues and strengths as much as that freak, Larry, diminished them. But in his forced courtesies to them he realized that his behavior was distorted as well. That's how fame distorts everyone in its orbit, he thought, chastising himself mildly for his habit of thinking in aphorisms. Christ, can't any of these people see I'm real?

"Why was that man, Larry, I think his name is . . ."

"Yes, Larry," Aaron said, glad to be of use.

"Why was he so angry at me?" Alters asked.

"He's just in a funk right now," Arnold said. "And he was drinking and for some stupid reason took it out on you. I'm sure he feels terrible about it already and will probably write you an elaborate apology in the morning."

"Is his life really as pathetic as it sounds?"

"When he's drinking, he thinks it is. But really, he's published a good amount of work, more than most of us, and he's got some good reviews, too. He does have some money problems right now, and he's a little insecure, but nothing he hasn't dealt with before."

"He mentioned something about not having a girlfriend."

"Maybe not now," Morty said, joining the conversation. "But he'll have one again soon."

"Well, the paradox of human motivation. Why did the not-so-young man attack me? In creative writing class, we're told to provide our characters with motivation, but it's always more mysterious in life, isn't it?"

"Amen," Morty said. Alters then asked if there was a phone he might use and Aaron directed him to one in the bedroom portion of the loft. On the way, Alters grabbed an abandoned drink by the punch bowl. Maybe he should have reassured Larry, or expressed an interest in his work, and all the ugliness could have been avoided. God, the guests had actually succeeded in making him feel guilty. Larry had started the fight and now they had him doubting himself. That's the thing about sycophants, he thought, as he closed the door to the room. They meant to make you feel totally supported but because you couldn't believe anything they said, you believed the opposite of what they said or you at least read between the lines and they ended up making you feel worse. Of course, there was no way for him to talk honestly with them, either, and that was the only thing that could make him feel better. It would shock them to know the kind of pain he was in, how on the edge he really was living, he thought with a bitter laugh as he sat down on the bed.

He decided he'd better call Tommy before he began to pity himself too much. With Tommy—an unemployed actor he'd met a few weeks ago and who'd become his first boyfriend—he could at least be quasi-honest. It was funny, when his interest in women began to fade he used to get relief from drinking but now, when he was trying to make a big decision, was on the verge of making it, instead of bringing relief, it just made everything worse. Things weren't simple, either, the way Tommy tried to make them seem. There was a lot to lose, and people who said it was fashionable now, at least in New York, were lying or deluding themselves. His fiction, his audience, his image were all straight and there was even serious talk of his getting one of the romantic leads in the next movie in his deal. How would everyone react to him as a gay writing star? Was there really such a creature today in supposedly enlightened America? Yet he felt he had to do it and sooner rather than later. Tommy was probably right about that.

It wasn't until the sixth ring that Tommy answered: Another childish trick to make him jealous? Alters cursed himself for giving him the key to his loft so soon, especially now that sex with him was only intermittently successful.

"Hi. I was just about to give up on you."

"Sorry, I was outside. It's snowing out! It's amazingly pretty, delicate snow, and I was just coming in when the phone rang. How are you?"

"Not tremendously good. I'm also more than a little high or low."

"Oh, I thought you said you didn't do that at parties."

"It's not a normal party."

"I told you you should have brought me with you."

"No, it's a normal party, almost all of the people are normal and all of them are straight, but this one frustrated macho writer in his late 30's started in on me about *Mercury.* Very sarcastic and nasty."

"He probably has the hots for you and doesn't even know it."

"I doubt it."

"The strain of your secret life is probably making you touchy, then."

"Anyway, he started a fight with me."

"Verbal?"

"No, physical."

"Are you all right?"

"Everyone's all right. It was broken up very quickly. I threw one punch and hit the host . . . by accident."

Tommy laughed for a second. "I told you I should go with you. Why are you so afraid of going to a party with me? Don't go without me again, O.K.?"

"O.K.," he said softly.

"When are you coming back? I miss you. I have the hots for you too."

"Tonight would be a very poor night for that."

"I didn't necessarily mean sex. I just want to see you and have fun with you."

Alters sighed. What a child Tommy was, albeit an adorable one.

"Did I say something wrong again, am I exasperating you?"

"No, no. I'm under a lot of pressure, that's all. I have to do an impossible amount of work."

"And keep up an impossible image."

"That's true too."

"No wonder."

"What? No wonder I can't 'do it' so well these days?"

"No, never mind. Just 'no wonder.' Just come home."

"So what is it you want to do so much if you don't expect to have sex?"

"There're lots of things to do. We could go outside and play in the snow. If it starts snowing harder, like it's supposed to, we could build a snowman together. How about that? Wouldn't you like to help me build a snowman?"

. . . .

Janice wasn't going to give up that easily. You didn't meet a Kenneth Alters every day, you didn't meet a Kenneth Alters in ten years, even in New York—not in her circle. And it was all going so promisingly. He was definitely looking at her breasts when that Larry moron made his psychotic bid for 15 minutes of party fame. Pathetic.

She thought of all the dreary readings, receptions, and parties she'd gone to faithfully over the years since she'd moved to New York from Florida. They said it was a golden time for women but men still held almost all the power positions in literary publishing. You still needed a male protector or male allies, but since she hadn't done an M.F.A., she'd missed the male teachers available at a writing program and at the parties all she'd met were a couple of poetry editors from really little magazines, one of whom she stupidly talked herself into sleeping with. But nothing like *Mercury,* nothing like Alters, who knew everyone in New York and who could get more or less anyone published if he endorsed them. She moved closer to the room where Alters was still on the phone and clenched her teeth. She saw the redhead who'd been trying to angle into her conversation with Alters before. She had her hair done up like Lucille Ball, and Janice gave her a dirty look. It's not a costume party, Lucy, she wanted to say, and it's not New Year's Eve yet either so why don't you drop the wig and clown makeup and try another approach. Pathetic. Janice kept her post directly in front of the door and turned her head away from Lucy. There was no reason now, nor any space, for Lucy to either cut in front of her or wait—no hope of conversation, either, as Janice had made plain, and eventually Lucy slunk away. Meanwhile, Janice had another drink and waited.

When Alters emerged from the bedroom, he had a look of purpose in his eyes that was temporarily disrupted when Janice stepped towards him.

"Hello again," she said, feeling immediately after he said hello back that he wanted to leave this foolish party as soon as possible.

"You were such a good sport to put up with that twit . . ."

For a moment Alters looked puzzled.

"You know, the jerk who attacked you."

"Oh, yes," Alters said smiling. "I'd forgotten about him and wasn't sure who you were talking about for a moment."

She laughed to show her empathy. "I meant to say it was generous of you to stay on at the party the way you did. I'm sure it meant a lot to the people here."

"Thank you."

"I know it was a thrill for me to meet you."

He thanked her again. Somewhat to his surprise, he felt the first stirring of an erection. Life was so complicated, he thought with a smile, as his eyes drifted down towards her breasts. Which, now that he thought about it, he'd enjoyed looking at before.

He managed to simultaneously keep talking to her, validate his erection, and do some quick thinking. From many parties before this one, he'd developed the technique of doing some of his most serious thinking while talking about completely unrelated things. He was wondering if she was the one who could end his sexual drought with women. More to the point, could he really afford to pass up the chance to find out with all it would mean to him professionally and personally? She certainly knew how to talk sweetly to him, and, at least with women, he found flattery was the most effective aphrodisiac, far more effective than pot, although delightful in combination with it. With Tommy, he was very rarely flattered; in fact, Tommy seemed to delight in thwarting him that way. He also didn't like the way his conversation with Tommy had ended and was still angry that Tommy had let the phone ring so many times before answering. Why didn't the answering machine pick up as it was programmed to do after four rings? Another trick of Tommy's to make him jealous? Or perhaps Tommy wasn't really out in the snow but was spreading his legs for some new stud he'd found in a bar, Alters thought, and getting back at me for not being invited to the party while risking my health, my life, in the process—the stupid, sex-addicted little prick.

She was telling him about her poetry now, then about her home state of Florida. She was awkward and naive, but trainable and definitely appealing. He made a few comments, asked a question, and before he knew it, she was telling him how magnificent the ending of his novel was, which made his erection stiffen another degree, until it reached its maximum potential.

She was definitely opportunity incarnate, and he decided he should certainly explore it—or try to. He could do that and still get back to Tommy tonight if he handled the situation right.

"You look like you're thinking about something real serious," she said.

"No, only that I was wondering if I'd stayed here long enough to be polite, so I could leave now."

"Oh."

"And also, if you'd like to leave, too, and go someplace else with me?" Her crestfallen look of a moment ago was replaced by a wide smile.

"Yes, I'd like that. Where would you like to go?"

"Oh, anywhere with you would be fun, I think," he said, and then drawing her close to him, kissed her a little more than briefly on the lips.

"What's your apartment like? Is it far away?" he said, after they separated. She already looked flushed, and he was encouraged. Perhaps she was one of those women who came very quickly.

"No, it's in the village. We could go there, though it's a mess right now," she said. "I just need to get my coat."

"Fine, marvelous," he said, smiling, before he realized that he needed to get his own coat as well.

. . . .

Was it in the elevator that he got his idea? He couldn't be sure as he stood behind the dumpster, on the street just to the left of the entrance to Aaron's loft. He seemed to have no memories on the elevator, he was just a shape falling then, and now he felt his whole body again as he crouched behind the dumpster watching the door. It was dark and cold but he felt no change of temperature or light while he waited, was even unaware of the snowflakes falling lightly but steadily on him as he crouched.

He thought he wouldn't have to wait long. After their fight how could Alters bear to stay there for any length of time? On the other hand, he couldn't really leave right away. Impeccable diplomat that he was, Alters would wait ten or fifteen minutes to show that he was not only unafraid but unruffled. But by then, after he joked and thanked a few people, the party would have exhausted what little use it had for him, and he would have to walk a block to get a cab. No taxis would be cruising down this little side street.

The door opened. For a split second he was stunned by the light and his hand went to his knife as he stared at the man just now walking under the street lamp. It was Morty—short, fat, balding Morty—walking home alone and still unpublished, still bookless after all these years, his snow-covered beret sitting absurdly on his head. He quickly ducked behind the dumpster until Morty slowly passed out of sight. It was then he first realized that the snow was falling on him too. The door opened two more times but it was people he didn't know or couldn't recognize except that they weren't Alters. Then he began to doubt that Alters would walk out alone. Why would he walk down the street like a plebeian when he could order a taxi to come to the door? With his money, taking a cab wasn't anything he'd fret about for a second. And what made him think that Alters would leave alone anyway? He remembered the rapt expression of Lady J's face while she listened to Alters. Why settle for her phone number when he could leave with her and salvage something pleasant from the evening? He imagined Alters making love with Lady J, then imagined him doing it with Debby. He'd intended to focus on these images for a moment to help keep up his resolve but found that, once in his mind, they stayed longer than he wanted. The snow was falling harder now. He imagined himself slowly being crowned with snow, head first, then over his dark clothes until he was white and immobile, a snow man with a knife, with the white, unwritten pages of a novel sitting at home as he realized that he must confront Alters again, that he couldn't endure the humiliation he'd suffered and must fight him in the snow. Realizing also that he must make Alters acknowledge him and apologize, that he must use whatever he needed to use and do whatever he needed to do to make Alters taste this dirty, relentless New York snow.

The door opened again and he saw them. It was like black magic. The image in his mind was prophetic, was happening now. Alters was walking with a brunette, and for a moment Larry couldn't tell if it was Lady J or Debby. He heard the steps get closer, like a bizarre dance routine reverberating on the frozen sidewalk—not enough snow on it yet to soften it. He saw Alters with his arm around the brunette, his hand sliding down to where her bottom was underneath her coat. He waited another set of steps and then stood up and away from the dumpster and made a running jump like a praying mantis. He had intended to say a sentence to him, something like, "Fight like a man, bitch!" but he was so astonished at the size of his jump and his feeling that he had done it like a praying mantis (that he was somehow insect-like now) that he didn't think he said anything—only emitted a strange sound, between a yell and a hiss.

Then the hitting began as they half-boxed, half-wrestled each other on the snow while the woman screamed. Alters hit him in the stomach, but Larry countered with an upper cut, followed by a left hook, and then he tackled and sat on him. He could see blood on Alters' face, while the woman yelled, "You'll go to jail for this. You're gonna do time."

That's all I've ever done, he said to himself. Then she ran down the street. Larry took out his knife and held it over Alters' dazed eyes. "This is for humiliating me, asshole. Now say you're sorry."

Half-conscious, Alters whispered something that sounded like "Sorry, Tommy." Larry wanted something better than that, but he realized that Lady J was probably already calling the cops, maybe had already called them, so he got off Alters' chest, still holding the knife in front of him.

"Don't follow me," he said, before he began running off as fast as he could down the dark narrow street.

BROOK

    The scariest thing about marrying a man is he gets to show you all your weaknesses one way or another and you half-believe him, too, if you're like me, no matter how much you argue with him. It's like you start seeing the world through his eyes even if they're bad eyes with a warped view. You can even consider yourself a feminist with more education than him and imagine you're the last person on earth who'd ever let any man brainwash you, but that's exactly what happens (actually you get half-brainwashed but that's enough, that's plenty) just from living with the guy, sleeping with him, hearing his rap so that no matter what dirt he does you, his voice is still in your brain and part of you believes that, if anything goes wrong, it's all your fault.

    In my case it was even more complicated than usual because Steven was just nice enough to me just long enough (as if he'd calculated it with some kind of perverse computer) to keep me perpetually hoping things would get better. That's why, when I found out he'd been cheating on me, I simply took it as a judgment that I wasn't satisfying him in bed. I didn't just cry about it either. I pored over sexual technique books and articles, I dieted when I didn't have to, I experimented endlessly with different hair styles, makeup, and clothes combinations. It was only during couples' therapy toward the end of our marriage that I realized Steven had been cheating on women his whole postpubescent life and that he'd done the same thing during his very short first marriage. On the one hand, it relieved me a bit from feeling like such a sexual failure (I'd even been secretly saving some money for breast implants, thinking that might make a difference). But it also forced me to see there was nothing to be done now since it was clearly a case of us having such different values or natures. Not only was infidelity inconceivable to me but so was promiscuity or even sleeping with someone before you loved them or thought you could—not that it's always so easy to know these things for sure. Steven used to kid me about being such a good girl and being so judgmental. I guess it's true. I can't lie. I can't even sell myself in an aggressive way like Steven did to get ahead in business, so that even though I had two years of college to his none (before I left school to marry him), he's way ahead of me career-wise. He also used to tell me to "lighten up" all the time, that the world (meaning him) needed laughter not tears, when in fact I love to laugh and do it all the time. I think the women comedians on cable TV are hilarious, for example, and so are the men. But I can't laugh at people being betrayed or hurt. I think you have to take people's feelings seriously or else you're a kind of emotional murderer.

Still the break from Steven wasn't easy for me. When the divorce became official sixteen months ago, I began occasionally having insomnia. The problem was I kept feeling things for him and not just anger either. I even began to wonder what it was like to live Steven's way, what would have to go on in his head to allow him to do it. With all the time alone I suddenly had, I'd think about this a lot, especially at night when it was hard to sleep.

I thought moving from Maryland to Florida would make things better but I fell into the habit of calling him when I couldn't sleep—first from Tallahassee, where I worked as an underpaid secretary in an insurance firm, then later from St. Petersburg, where I worked in a jewelry store. All these conversations took place after we were legally divorced and he was undoubtedly amusing some panting creature with his free hand while he spoke to me. I couldn't bring myself to even say my name when I called him, but the guilty bastard would say, "Doreen Doreen, that you?" and I'd start talking, sometimes on the pretext of asking some financial question, other times just talking about whatever was in my head. But always it ended with my yelling at him that he'd ruined my life, that I was a decent, ethical woman working way under her potential and level of education and he was a no-good male whore who'd scarred me forever—or words to that effect. I give him credit for listening to me—I was always the one who yelled first and who ended by hanging up on him.

I was quite miserable and panicky then, but time can be your ally in that kind of situation. After a while the need to call him started to fade, and soon I started calling a lot less and sleeping a lot better.

When I settled in Bayside I was already sleeping pretty well and was really feeling substantially better in spite of my even-lower-than-usual-paying job as a guard ("in security" is the term we're supposed to use) for the town library. But everything changed after I met Brook. Hard to believe that a single day with one man could screw me up so much at my age that I went right back to insomnia again, as if that was what I was married to now. The only ways I could get relief were from sleeping pills or massive doses of TV. And when the pills wore off or I couldn't stand TV anymore there was a good chance I'd see that indescribable expression on Brook's face while he was giving me the money and I'd think if I could only find the words to describe the expression I could get some kind of control over it and make it disappear. Sometimes, also, I'd become convinced that Brook was planning to do something desperate to see me again and that while he seemed so in control of things when he was with me he was liable to snap at any moment in some unimaginably weird way.

Leaving work yesterday afternoon I thought I might snap myself. The sharp green grass of the library lawn pointed up at me like a row of spears. I couldn't decide which road to walk down to get to the small beach house I'm renting on Clinton Street. It was like choosing between alternate routes in a long, twisting cemetery. This time I went by the marina, where I've never heard any cars. It was so quiet I started an inventory of the different kinds of noises I could still hear. There were the palm trees moving slightly but not quite silently in the breeze, there were the muted repetitive birdcalls I normally wouldn't be aware of, and then, of course, the sounds my feet made on the street.

I saw a seagull cleaning itself and thought how everything in nature is always grooming itself, as if preparing for some grand inspection, and I thought of the clothes I had already bought with some of the money

Brook gave me. Then I noticed someone standing on one of the docks looking at the water. Damned if it wasn't Brook, himself, stooped and quiet like one of the palm trees. When I watched a little longer, I saw a melancholic, almost tragic expression on his face. Maybe he really did love his wife a lot, I thought, thinking of Steven wistfully for a second, or maybe he somehow knew I was watching and it was just a trick to make me sorry for him by making me think he was depressed because I wouldn't see him.

In bed that night I kept seeing the image of Brook staring at the water until I finally got up and decided to take a walk. But as soon as I put on my slip I stopped. My spontaneous trips into town hadn't really worked out in the past—in fact they'd ended up being pretty disastrous. There was the completely fruitless time I spent in the town bars, which didn't result in a single date or even any moment worthy of memory, and then, of course, there were my Saturday afternoons at the Ambassador pool where I'd met Brook—which had begun with the same kind of restless feeling I felt now.

I didn't want to think of him again but couldn't really help it. It was like a curtain rising in a play I was forced to watch still one more time as my whole pre-pool routine came back to me. I saw again how I selected my best bathing suit, a black two-piece—a little revealing but certainly not vulgar—then the extra time I spent on make-up trying to get that full-lip look that's so in vogue these days, then taking my white beach coat and selecting the right pair of sunglasses before heading toward the Ambassador. (The security was pretty lax there, so it was much easier for a non-guest to use the pool.) I always chose a chaise lounge away from any women, fearing they'd be too nosy since I not only didn't live at the Ambassador but didn't know anyone who did. My idea was that I might meet a nice man, as the Ambassador was part of a group of luxury condominiums overlooking the bay and you had to be pretty successful to live there.

The first three times I didn't meet any men and the only people who talked to me were women. One of them asked me if I were the guard at the public library and I put my sunglasses back on and said I wasn't.

"Well, you look just like her," the woman said.

I'd leave the pool those afternoons feeling cheated and sad but still encouraged enough to come back. The last time, a man sat next to me but just as he started talking one of the pool security people approached me.

"Excuse me, ma'am," he said, with more than a trace of contempt. "Could I see your pool card?"

The man in the chaise lounge next to me suddenly said, "Ken, she's my guest." It was just like a scene in the movies, as the security man tipped his golf cap and went away.

"Thanks," I said.

"My name's Brook and it's my pleasure."

"Hi, I'm Doreen."

Immediately, I looked at his hands and didn't see a ring. Then I looked at the rest of him and saw a heavyish man who was probably at least sixty and seemed to have trouble smiling, as if some teeth were missing, which I realized later was indeed the case. Still, he'd already been kind, so what harm could it do to find out more about him? Brook was not at all shy about talking. He was a semiretired businessman who played the market and did some consulting here and there. His son was finishing Harvard Medical School and his daughter was married to a successful lawyer in Miami. For five years now he'd been a widower—a heart attack having taken his wife "in her prime," as he put it. He still stayed in the same condominium in which she'd died because it felt right somehow to be close to her, although he also had just closed on a home in Miami and figured he'd be spending a good deal of time there to be near his daughter.

"The market can do wonderful things for people," he said, and began telling me about his financial triumphs.

A couple of hours passed and nearly everyone else left the pool. There was an awkward pause and I began to feel confused. I guess I was hurt that he'd asked me so few questions about myself, but, on the other hand, he did seem the kind of person I would never meet at the library. Also there was something in his tone of voice and manner, so confident and reassuring, that I found appealing. When he asked me if I'd like to see his condominium, I said sure.

Maybe he's only in his late or even middle fifties, I thought, as we rode the elevator. He was wearing a white short-sleeve shirt over his navy-blue bathing suit and white tennis shoes, and looked vaguely athletic. He took my hand briefly to lead me out of the elevator but I didn't think anything of it. Men of his generation behave with that kind of courtesy and I sort of enjoyed it.

A flick of his key and his condominium billowed out in front of us. He escorted me into the living room, than excused himself for a minute, telling me to make myself at home. It really was getting more and more like a movie. There I stood on his thick rose carpet, the sun starting to set over the bay. On the walls were oil paintings of his wife and children but also works of art that looked to be legitimate. I could certainly see that his furniture was. I sat down on a gold-and-magenta sofa facing the water. Overhead a chandelier shone so brightly it seemed to be made of diamonds.

When he came out (still in his bathing suit) I noticed something different. He was smiling broadly as he approached me and I realized that he'd put in his false teeth. He set a bottle of wine on the table beside me and offered me a glass. I noticed that he'd put on a generous amount of cologne as well. I liked that he was being so genteel and thoughtful, but I was also feeling somewhat uneasy. While we were drinking he started talking about his wife.

"I can't begin to tell you how much I loved her, how difficult it's been to go on without her, but go on I must, even though sometimes the world doesn't seem to want me to."

"What do you mean?"

"Just that it's difficult for a gentleman to meet a woman he cares for, especially in my case where I don't feel ready for an older woman yet . . . May I ask if you're married?"

For a second I hesitated; so many times the answer had been "yes."

"No, I'm not." He poured another glass of wine.

"Of course you're a terribly attractive woman, and you're so young. I'm sure you don't have any problems meeting people."

"I've had trouble meeting the right kind," I said, as I took a substantial swallow of my drink.

"But what could the average man offer you? Is there anything, for instance, that I could offer you because I'd love to be your right kind. I find you very appealing in every way."

His sudden aggression (like a salesman, I thought) stunned me. I finished my drink but couldn't think of anything to say.

"Really, anything I could offer you I'd be happy to give if you'll just tell me what it is."

"Whatever you think," I mumbled, feeling foolish. He rose from the sofa and I was struck by how strong he looked.

Then I was in his old, strong arms, not resisting him or even thinking about why I wasn't. On the way to his bedroom, still in his grasp, I thought I couldn't speak because I'd spoken so little during the whole afternoon. So instead of asking him to stop I found myself concentrating on the mechanical things I had to do to make it happen as smoothly as possible, which considering his age might not be easy. His weight was one problem. I had to position myself so I wouldn't be crushed while he kissed me. Also, his mouth didn't taste that good, and I was actually relieved when he started kissing my breasts. I watched him for a moment, old man at a baby's task, then looked out above him at the blue and rose room filled with family pictures and paintings, half-hidden in the dim light.

When he was done with his foreplay I took off my suit—anything to help him, I was thinking—and as I suspected, it was a little difficult for him, especially with his condom. It didn't really bother me to touch him, but when it was over I was choking back tears. Brook looked at me guiltily for a moment, then excused himself. I've got to get out of here as fast as I can, I thought, and I was already dressed and ready to leave by the time he came out of the bathroom and intercepted me in the hallway. He was wearing his bathing suit and flip-flops and holding his shirt in his hand.

"You're not leaving are you?" he said, looking genuinely concerned.

"I have to."

"But why?"

"I didn't expect this . . . any of this . . . I'm late."

"Will I see you again?"

I looked at his eyes and saw how blue and imploring they were and didn't know what to say.

"If you're feeling badly about what happened it doesn't have to happen next time. We could just be friends—though I won't deny I'm deeply attracted to you."

Then he withdrew something from his shirt pocket and pressed it into my hands.

"Please take this and enjoy it, buy something with it. It would mean a lot to me."

I opened my hands, which were trembling in spite of my efforts to stop them, and saw two hundred-dollar bills.

"Thanks," I said softly. "I'll call you. I have to go." I squirmed past him in the hallway and opened the door with the money now crumpled in my left fist.

Somehow, I made it to the elevator walking in a straight line like an automaton, but as soon as I stepped inside I closed my eyes and saw orange, like I did when I was seven years old and was first stung by a bee. When I got out of the elevator I was shaking all over, more out of anger than fear. What had I done? I'd not only slept with the old egotist the first day I'd met him, I'd taken his money, too, just like a call girl. I'd acted no better than Steven and worse than my quasi-nymphomaniac sister Lorraine ever did.

A few days later, I was able to think about what happened more calmly, and typically I began to rationalize it, probably hoping to let myself off the hook a little. The defense attorney in my head rose up and spoke first, saying when Brook asked you what he could offer you, your answer had been vague, but you certainly hadn't asked for money. Then the prosecutor stood up and noted that I couldn't deny that I'd accepted it without a word of protest. If you were lovers or friends, my prosecutor continued, who'd done it once in a moment of wine-induced weakness, then what he'd done was simply to give you a present, albeit in a crude way. But if you were friends, why can't you bring yourself to see him again and why have you repeatedly fantasized about ripping up the money in front of him or sending it back torn in a thousand pieces inside an envelope? Instead you deposited it in your savings account where it got all mixed up with the money you've worked for, and later you used some of that money to buy yourself a dress.

When Brook called two days later and invited me to lunch at the most expensive restaurant in Bayside, I came up with an excuse. It was all I could manage to stay politely neutral on the phone and to tell him I'd call back. But so far I hadn't. Meanwhile he'd called three more times, and each time I had to come up with a lie and then I'd feel more nervous about the whole situation. It reached the point where I didn't always answer the phone and dreaded even hearing it ring. That was ironic since not too long ago I thought the telephone ring was one of the most exciting sounds in the world. When I was first going out with Steven, I remember making little shrieking noises when the phone rang, almost like I was having sex, and then when it turned out to be him I'd be ecstatic. We'd talk for hours and sometimes he could make me feel like we actually were making love while we spoke. Steven was smooth with words then, or rather, I hadn't yet developed the ability to sort out the false ones.

Last night when the phone rang I didn't answer it. I was sure it was Brook, which made me wonder if soon he wouldn't just show up at my door somehow, wallet in hand, since like a fool I'd told him where I live.

Another paradox: if I had taken the phone off the hook and kept it off long enough he might begin to worry. He'd have the operator verify my busy signal, discover there was trouble on the line, and use that as a pretext to appear at my door claiming he was concerned. But to continue to let it ring as I'd been doing invited the same possibility, though his pretext for coming over wouldn't have been quite as solid. Did Brook worry about solid pretexts? The truth is, when you have a tremendous money advantage over someone you don't need to worry about pretexts—you just act. Of course I could have just left, but I was afraid Brook might have been outside watching my house from his car and could easily spot me. Brook had the speed advantage too.

It's funny, at the library I often stand at my post by the door without moving for an hour at a stretch, but here in my own home I was pacing like an hysteric. Finally I picked up the phone and started to call Steven but I stopped before I pressed the last digit. I could never tell him about Brook, at least not without repercussions. I thought it would hurt him pretty badly, too, to listen to it. Like all philanderers Steven has a fragile ego. Besides, he'd just call me a hypocrite or a whore, and I'm not sure I could contradict him with much conviction. It would probably end with my hanging up on him and finding myself back at square one.

Then I thought about calling my sister Lorraine in Seattle but quickly rejected that idea. We used to be incredibly close and could tell each other everything and laugh about everything too. But when my marriage broke down I suddenly started thinking she was a female version of Steven. We had some fights about her ultra-active sex life and then grew somewhat apart. Speaking to either of my parents was even more out of the question. I'd gotten it down to four calls a year with them and figured they preferred it that way too. After all their cold years together in Wisconsin they've sort of grown strangely compatible in their semiavoidance of each other, like two adjacent icicles, relieved their daughters were each getting into trouble a thousand miles away from them.

It would be ideal to talk to someone from around here but I didn't know who that would be, Brook being the only person who'd taken any interest in me since I'd been in Bayside. The upshot of all this was I decided to call Steven again just to try to steady my nerves a little, but what do you know, his line was busy, and when I verified it with the long distance operator I found there was "trouble on the line." That's no trouble, I almost said to the operator, that's Steven exercising his glands again with some luckless lady.

I left the house then, barely remembering to take my pocketbook with me, and started walking straight down the road. It was a typical hot Florida night but I felt chilled as if my flesh was somehow missing and I'd been left as hollow as a scarecrow—an easy mark for Brook.

Without planning to I'd walked back to the marina where I'd last seen Brook and a shiver ran through me. It looked the same as it always did, the empty benches, the oversized streetlamps huge and bent like the necks of dinosaurs, the light reflected on the unmoving water, the boats not moving either, as if all this were part of a painting instead of nature. Across a wooden bridge, about one hundred yards from me, was a pay phone, right next to one of those dinosaur streetlamps with its hideously bright oversized light. I could use my Sprint card, I thought, the only one I'm not overdrawn on, and call Steven again (he'd probably be through with sex by then, and very possibly might have already sent the woman home), and in some way, in spite of everything, it would help me calm down. I was on my way to do this, walking over the bridge, when I felt an extreme anxiety as if I were in the rifle sights of a marksman about to blow me away. I kept walking at the same pace and was almost halfway across the bridge when I heard an engine's hum, turned, and saw a car trailing me, the driver's head out the window. It was Brook. He said, "Doreen, are you all right?"

I looked at the car, not knowing where to move, and stayed completely still as the car moved nearer until I realized it was a sky-blue Cadillac.

"Hi," he said.

"Hi."

"Going anywhere special?"

"No. Just walking."

"Want some company? Why don't you hop in?"

I pointed ineffectually toward the phone or maybe I just looked in that direction and then I said either "O.K." or something like it, and the next thing I knew I was sitting beside him on his thick leather seat. Brook started driving in the general direction of the beach. After a minute of silence he said, "I've missed you." Then he looked at me, but I avoided him and stared straight ahead at the night where it was too dark to see much of anything except the light of the lamps themselves and the little bright spaces they created on the ground.

"I've been calling you but I guess you haven't been in."

"Oh," I said.

"Don't you have an answering machine?"

"I don't know enough people here to need a machine."

"I see," Brook said, softly. I still hadn't met his eyes yet and was just looking straight ahead. When he reached the end of Clinton he turned left on Ocean Street, which runs along the length of the town beach.

"There's a moon out tonight. I thought you might like to see it over the water."

I remembered the ocean paintings in his condominium and the shining chandelier, but I didn't say anything. He continued driving slowly, not saying anything either. I was thinking there was no way I could talk to Steven again without telling him about Brook. It was just a question of whether I'd have to tell him about the one-night stand and taking the money, or something additional that could come from tonight. It didn't matter that we were divorced, that I owed him nothing, that my life was my own now. I had to tell him, even if it hurt him, even if I couldn't ever judge him the same way again.

"Doreen, I can't help feeling that I've done something that's really hurt you. I wish you'd tell me what it is."

I kept silent, my eyes looking straight ahead.

"You haven't called me back; you can't even bring yourself to look at me," he said, stopping the car, then turning to look directly at me. I could hear the bay through his open window, the birds squawking in the distance. We had stopped near the casino—white and pink and lit up. Beside it a pier extended a couple of hundred yards into the bay. People were still fishing on it by the same type of dinosaur lamps they have at the marina.

"Doreen, will you talk to me?" His voice sounded soft and humble like an echo of itself.

"O.K. I'll talk. It's only fair, I guess." My eyes finally located the pay phone in the splash of light outside the casino. It was crazy how bright it was, like they were trying to expose and capture everyone who was passing by in a prison of light.

"Until that day at your place I'd never slept with anyone unless I loved them or really seriously thought I could. I'm not blaming you for that. I did it, I went against what I believed, and that's what hurt me. I don't know why I did it. I don't know if I was trying to get back at my husband or maybe trying to forgive him but now I have to tell him what I did . . ."

"Wait a minute. I thought you were divorced for over a year now."

"I am. It's just that we still talk and I've been judging him so long on the way he lives and now I can't. And when I took the money from you, that really punctuated what I did. I'll have to tell him that, too."

"But you're divorced. I don't see why you have to tell him anything at all."

"Don't you understand? Don't you have any kind of code that you follow?" I said, finally turning in my seat and looking straight at him. He looked sad and flustered and suddenly older than I'd realized.

"Sure I do. But at my age I've become more flexible about things like codes. The main thing to me is just warmth or caring. But about the money, that was wrong. I've never done that before and I regret it. I didn't do that to insult you, God knows, just the opposite. I did it hoping it would make you want to see me again."

I saw something like tears in his eyes and looked away. I remembered one time (it may have been the only time) when my father apologized for yelling at me. I was about eight years old and when I saw tears in his eyes I was shocked—he not being a demonstrative man—and began crying myself. I felt like that now and didn't want to, so I tried to focus on the outrage I felt when Brook had handed me the money.

"You remember when I said that I'd understand if you just wanted to be friends? I meant that. That would make me more than happy. I've found it's almost as hard to find a friend as a girlfriend."

"But we began by sinning . . . against ourselves and each other. That's not the way for a friendship to start." Brook shook his head and mumbled "no."

"Will you think about it, though?" he said softly.

"Yeah, I'll think about it. But right now I have to use the telephone."

"I'll wait here and drive you back."

"No need."

"It's more than two miles from your house."

"Don't you know women love to exercise?" I said as I finally opened the door and went straight to the phone.

But the call turned out to be hard to make. I got about halfway through Steven's number three or four times but hung up each time. Meanwhile Brook was circling around the parking lot in his car. I knew he wouldn't leave without trying once more to drive me home. He was staying about a hundred feet away. When his path took him to the edge of the sand I squinted my eyes and made his car look like a boat and then a fish coming out of the bay. He might be manipulative and talk too much, but there was also something nice about him. I kept an eye on him and decided to call my parents, thinking I might like to speak to my father. But I hung up before I finished that number too. Instead I called my sister in Seattle.

"Lorraine, that you?"

"Doreen?"

"You got some time for this?"

"Sure I do. How are you, girl?"

"Lorraine, I've wanted to talk to you for so long. It's good to hear your voice again."

I told her I was sorry I hadn't called before, that I was an idiot to have always judged her so much, and she made a nervous little joke. Then I told her there was a guy with a big crush on me driving his Cadillac in circles outside the phone booth hoping to drive me home. An older man I'd already slept with the first day I met him. I told her about him giving me the money and she said that didn't sound too bad. The way she said it made me laugh, and I began to breathe easier. "No, it isn't that bad, it's just very strange," I said, watching his car start another circle under the moonlight. I saw him driving at an even pace, beginning his arc again by the edge of the sand, his car lights neither high nor low, and I thought the next time he swooped by I'd wave to him or maybe shout "Hello."

BARRY AND ELLIOT

Elliot tiptoed into the living room, looked over his shoulder at Barry's body stretched out on his futon and could scarcely believe his good luck. It had only been two weeks ago that he'd futilely tried to locate Barry, as he had a few times each year or so, via the telephone operators in New York. Of course, there was no reason to assume that Barry was still in New York. After 11 years he could be anywhere, he could be out of America or even dead. That was beginning to happen to a number of people Elliot knew. In the last year alone he'd heard that a woman he'd slept with for most of a summer twenty years ago had died in a car accident and later that a casual male friend from his childhood, but one he still had a clear memory of, had died of AIDS. Maybe, by telling him nothing, the operators were doing him a favor, giving him a sign lest he continue to pursue his long-lost friend and find out something at the end of it all that would be shocking and horrible.

Then a week later the miracle call came late at night. It was Barry's unmistakably raspy voice speaking to him imploringly from Paris. It was an emergency, a crisis, but what else would it be that would make Barry call after eleven years of silence? The fact is they barely discussed the years when they hadn't talked there was so much to talk about now.

Barry's story was typically impossibly tangled. His mother had died three years ago from a failed kidney, his father had robbed him and his mother while she was ill, an art dealer had ripped him off of $30,000, and he might sue his former psychiatrist. Could Elliot call him back and listen to his story, please? Barry was calling from a hotel phone. He had no home now, and though he expected a large sum of money in a few months, right now he had nothing.

Elliot made the overseas call—and listened for almost two hours but understood little except that Barry was coming to America to track down his father, Joe, to get back the $120,000 he'd stolen. Could Elliot find him a place to stay in New York?

He felt slightly stung by yet another reminder from Barry of the provinciality of his life. When they were high school seniors in Brookline Barry used to mock Boston in the months before setting off for Columbia and "the real world of New York." Now that they were about to be reunited and Barry was leaving Paris, he seemed to be judging Philadelphia as too provincial, as well, to help him in his far flung operations. Moreover, by being asked who he knew in New York, Elliot was reminded that his meager circle of mostly academic friends scarcely extended beyond the Philadelphia city limits. Nevertheless, Elliot said he'd try to find him a place in New York and assured him he could always stay with him in Philadelphia if all else failed.

"I hope I won't have to do that to you," Barry said. "I know how important it is for you to be alone."

That's not true, Elliot had said to himself, or it's only half true. Certainly it wasn't true since his divorce two years ago.

"After I get it done," Barry continued on the phone from Paris, "and I've got to get it done in a short time or my life is over, you can visit me and stay in my apartment and we can party in Paris, Elliot. We can party in Paris, capiche?"

"Why aren't you in your apartment now?"

"They've turned the power off. They say I owe them thousands of dollars. My landlady is a professional bitch and anti-Semite. She wants me out because I'm Jewish. It's in litigation."

That sounded like the Barry he remembered. I think, therefore I litigate. Barry's adult life had been dominated by the courts. It had begun in his early twenties when Myrna, Barry's mother, won a palimony suit, which like a magic plant began sprouting other lawsuits along with the desire not to pay the I.R.S. any of the money they won. Though they were certainly never what Elliot would consider criminals, they did do some highly unusual things to avoid paying taxes, which Elliot now had to admit appealed to his sense of drama. What wasn't appealing was when they wanted him to help them in their schemes. Once they tried to sell him their loft in SoHo and then have him sell it back to them the next day. Another time Elliot agreed to store some paintings for a summer which Barry had stolen from his father's New York apartment. Barry wanted to use them as negotiating chips to get back the money Joe had stolen from him during Joe's visit to Paris. (Years later, it was Elliot's refusal to cooperate with one of these schemes that led to their falling out.)

Though Myrna had divorced him shortly after Barry was born, Joe kept reappearing in Barry's life, in part because Barry kept seeking him out. Elliot had only met Joe once when he and Barry were about twelve but found him frightening even then. Barry's official position was that his father was a psychopath and that he hated him for what he'd done to Myrna. But often when he talked about him his eyes lit up and the admiration for his father's "genius ability to con people," to bed women, "to make and lose and make a million dollars again and again," even for his supposed ties to the Mafia—was pathetically unmistakable.

Barry's parents had always been the overwhelming influence in his life. Fortunately, he had a lot of Myrna's tenderness, but he clearly reflected as well his dark legacy from Joe. Despite claiming various highly dubious literary triumphs, Barry never worked at any job and seemed content with being supported by Myrna. It was also odd that, despite saying he'd slept with many women (a few of whom Elliot had met), by his own admission Barry had never fallen in love. Whenever he acknowledged this it seemed to be of no more consequence to him than admitting he'd never written a haiku or a Villanelle. But maybe it hurt him more than he pretended. That was possible. Even more disturbing was that Barry had begun lying as his father did. At least they seemed like lies. First there were his preposterous tales about his sexual conquests—Barry claimed to have slept with everyone from Faye Dunaway to Susan Sontag—then it was about all the famous literary people he knew, and finally about his books that were always just about to be published. In his call from Paris, Barry claimed that he had two books coming out in the next few months, a novel and a collection of critical essays, and a six- or seven-figure deal promised for the one after that. Elliot, a playwright who had published enough to get tenure but not nearly as much as he'd hoped, was always highly skeptical about these stories but could never disbelieve them enough to be entirely free of jealousy. It was deeply ironic to be jealous of someone's fantasies, he realized, but there it was.

And there was Barry in his living room after all these years, his stay in New York lasting little more than a week for reasons that Elliot still didn't understand. He walked closer to him, saw the painting Barry had recovered from New York and next to that the urn that contained his mother's ashes. "Myrna Rosenthal," it said on the golden urn, with the dates of her life. After staring at it Elliot shuddered a little. Beside the urn was a polaroid of Myrna sitting next to Barry on a sofa—smiling in her Sutton Place apartment. She was truly the only woman Barry had ever loved, Elliot thought, and he had loved her unstintingly. Elliot had been fond of her himself and, after bending down to look at the photograph, tiptoed by it. Then he remembered that Barry would often sleep till 12:00 or 12:30 and that ordinary noise could rarely wake him. Asleep, Barry looked dignified yet oddly innocent. The black beard that circled his face was now dotted with gray as were the temples of his coarse, jet black hair, where there was a dangerously thin section on top like a shallow circle of thin ice in a pond. But everything about his appearance would change when he woke up. With his eyes open—his wild, liquid-filled eyes that in some lights looked sea blue, in others, depending on how much their brown pupils expanded, piercing green—Barry often looked preternaturally intense, like a figure in a Van Gogh painting or like Van Gogh himself. Elliot thought of himself as probably the more conventionally good looking man, but a part of him had always envied Barry's fiercely singular face.

. . . .

"I like what you've done with your life," Barry said, gesturing expansively toward Elliot. They were sitting by the picture window in the living room facing each other. Barry, still in impressive shape, was wearing an elegant gray shirt and smartly matching silver-gray pants. His cheese-eating outfit, he called it, that he'd bought in Paris. Although he was broke he still had some expensive clothes from all those years that he and Myrna had money and lived in Sutton Place and the Hamptons. In his frayed navy blue pants and Phillies tee shirt, Elliot felt drab and almost invisible, as he softly said "thank you."

"And I'm deeply grateful for your letting me stay here."

"Don't mention it."

"It's very generous of you after all those years . . . when we didn't speak."

"I thought about you a lot. A couple of weeks before you called I even tried to find out if you were still in New York."

"I know we each had our reasons for what happened."

"We don't need to talk about it, do we? There's enough going on in the present isn't there?"

"Of course. I just want to say that the reasons I had no longer apply. That's what I meant about liking what you've done with your life."

Elliot felt himself bristle slightly but held his tongue. He thought Barry was subtly implying that he, Elliot, had been selfish then but had become more giving now. Selfish, to have refused to break the law and jeopardize his life! But what did it matter? Barry always had to be one up on him and he was probably the same way toward Barry. He looked into Barry's eyes again.

"After I get it done I'll reimburse you for all of this," Barry said.

"I don't care about that."

"I'm going to have to make some long distance phone calls to the lawyers who are working on my cases, to the private detectives in New York who found my father, which I'll tell you about, and then a few calls—and I'll really try to keep the number down—to some people in Paris."

"That's O.K."

"And I'm going to have to ask you for a couple of hundred bucks so I can feel like a man. I'm down to my last three dollars, Elliot. In New York I had to spend a night on the street, then I had to walk here from the train station with all my things in that incredible heat. I couldn't even afford a cab."

"I'm sorry I wasn't in or I would have paid for the cab. I had to see these people about a play that I'm coaching."

"Is this for your college? You're not teaching summer school again, are you?"

"No, nothing like that," Elliot said laughing. "Though we may end up doing a performance there in the fall, if I can work out the details, but no, it has nothing to do with my school. We're just a group of people who used to meet once or twice a month to read through plays—Philadelphia has lots of reading and writing groups like that—and then we decided we'd like to start performing in some little way, since most of the people in the group had some kind of theatrical experience or knew people who did and . . . voilà."

"Are they doing one of your plays?"

"No. We're doing *The Glass Menagerie* and I'm trying my hand at directing it. Maybe I'll be more successful at that," Elliot said laughing. "But, no. I wouldn't presume to suggest they do one of my plays."

"You should. You have an important talent. You should presume."

"Thank you. That means a lot."

"I've always believed that. Obviously I haven't read the work you've done lately and I'm not in the state of mind where I really could now until I get my money and my life back . . ."

"Of course."

"But you know I've always believed you have a first rate talent and after I get it done, after I get the money that was stolen from my mother and me, I'll get your plays translated and published in France. I'll send them directly to my publishers and it will all be taken care of."

Elliot looked at Barry closely trying to guess how much of this might be true.

"And I'll get them performed too."

"How will you do that?"

"Arriane, my lover—who I met just before my crisis started and I had to come to America—is considered one of the three or four most promising young directors in Paris."

"This is the same one you told me about on the phone whose apartment you stayed at?"

"Arriane, of course. Just get your manuscript together and maybe a few reviews and I'll do it as soon as I get it done here and get my life back in Paris, O.K.?"

•••••••••

After Barry had gone out for a coffee, Elliot began compiling his papers. It had been so long since anyone had asked to read his work, much less the reviews about it, that he felt both grateful and unusually energized. But after he'd selected his best plays and reviews, updated his resume slightly, and put the material together in a folder in its most effective order, he began to wonder just what he was getting excited about. Of course it would be wonderful to be published in French and performed in Paris. He would fly there to witness it. But all this excitement ultimately was based on Barry's really having the kind of power and influence he said he did. The biggest reason he'd always doubted Barry's literary triumphs was simply because his books never appeared any more than Faye Dunaway or any of his other luminous conquests ever showed up on Barry's arm. On the other hand, he had seen just enough of Barry's very well-written articles in his twenties and met just enough of his women to believe some of his stories were possible, and besides all those lies were years ago. Barry was forty-three now and he was promising Elliot something that he wanted. Would he lie about something like that? It was one thing to be troubled, to be overwhelmed by troubles, which could and probably did happen to everyone at times and had clearly happened to Barry. But it was another thing entirely to plant false hopes in someone who was starved for them. He couldn't believe Barry, who had made many mistakes in his life but never the mistake of cruelty, could do that to him.

He began watching and listening to Barry with a little more detachment in the next few days, feeling vaguely like a market analyst charting the daily fluctuations of a stock in an attempt to determine its true worth. Thus when he saw Barry drinking either three or four straight vodkas a night, or a bottle of wine, the stock went down several points, and the stock slid further as he noticed the decline in Barry's hygiene. Barry had never been neat but also never anything like this. Every morning Elliot found a trail of wine stains on the kitchen floor and counters, as well as doughnut parts, potato chip parts, food bags and wrappers, and as often as not chocolate from a candy bar crusted on the kitchen or living room floors. He brought this up half jokingly to Barry, showing him where the sponge and trash bags were, but it seemed to make no difference and the mess continued. Barry's bathroom hygiene was even more appalling—the toilet seat was stained and the floor area around it stank from urine. Moreover, after a few days he couldn't help noticing that Barry's underpants were filthy. How could he stand to walk around in them when Elliot couldn't bear to look at them? Finally he simply gave him a new pair. He was beginning to notice a smell that was pervading the apartment. He opened the windows, but it was so hot outside he couldn't leave them open for long, so he sprayed the apartment with air freshener. Still the bad smell was so insidiously pervasive that this own underpants smelled as if Barry had been wearing them. Quickly Elliot began stuffing his pillow cases with clothes to do laundry. When he got near the green towel in the bathroom that Barry used, he felt nauseated from its stench and the stock plummeted further.

That night at dinner, at the only decent French restaurant in Philadelphia that Elliot could afford, things got better. Barry was funny and extremely charming as he used to be. He made the waitress laugh, and he made Elliot laugh with his clever analysis of silly French attitudes about America and vice versa.

"After I finish the book about my mother I'd like to write a light little book, a soufflé of a book about this transatlantic social silliness. Sometimes I think my head is going to burst because I have the ideas—detailed ideas—for about twenty different books inside it."

When the topic shifted to writers Barry made a brilliant analysis of Gore Vidal's strengths and limitations as a writer, and the stock rallied a few more points. It was vintage Barry—twenty-seven-year-old Barry—when Elliot used to marvel and be envious of the essays he'd published in the *New Republic* and the *Village Voice*. It was such a close and insightful critique and dealt so intimately with Vidal's sensibility and life that he felt prepared to accept that Barry had indeed become good friends with Vidal in Europe.

"If only there wasn't a catastrophe going on in Gore's life right now he'd lend me the money I need in a minute and he'd get twice as much money back a year after my next book comes out. Then I wouldn't have to bother about my psychopathic father. By the way, did I tell you I found him?"

"No, you didn't," Elliot said in a startled voice.

Barry nodded with a cryptic smile and Elliot began to doubt him. "When was this?"

"Right before I came to see you. The P.D.'s tracked him down. He's living in a dump in Jersey City. They offered to scare him a little but I decided it would be better to go there myself and confront him about the money."

"Why didn't you tell me about this right away?"

"I didn't want to upset you; I didn't want to bring up such a heavy thing like that right away after not seeing you for so long. But maybe I should have. You're not hurt, are you?"

"No, of course not."

"Because I'd never hurt you."

"No, it's fine."

"Anyway I did confront the bastard and obviously I didn't get my hundred and twenty thousand."

"What happened?"

"He doesn't have it. He's poor and sick and seventy-three years old. He has cancer, too."

"How did he react when he saw you?"

Barry paused, as he rarely did, before saying, "Stoically. I took a chance that he'd be there and didn't call or write first. I just showed up at his door and waited. He drove back from his errand, parked the car, crossed the street, looked up and saw me. He said, 'How did you find me?' in a pretty deadpan voice. He kept his cool. I'll give him that."

"Unbelievable!"

"Elliot, this is a man who's dealt drugs, forged and sold fake paintings, and made and lost millions of dollars. This is a man who was in the Mafia, a man who's probably ordered dozens of hits, capiche?"

Barry's dramatic catalogue made Elliot laugh for a moment in spite of himself. Barry also laughed. "It is like an insane soap opera, isn't it?" Barry said, smiling. "Here," he said, taking a crumpled piece of stationery out of his pants pocket. "Take a look at this. Ever seen one of these before?"

Elliot took the paper, carefully unfolded it, and abandoned his shepherd's pie to read it. It was a report from a private detective agency in New York documenting Joe's address, phone number, aliases, previous places of business, and known associates. It was all unmistakably authentic, Elliot thought.

"So how do things stand now between you two?"

"He says if he had it he'd give it to me but he doesn't have it. He's broke and he's tired, but he's going to try to pull off a deal for me in the next few days. See, I have a lot of information on him—things I can document that can put him away, and he knows it. I'm going to give him a deadline to get it done for me or I'll turn him in—that's all. Remember, the man's a monster. He beat my mother while they were married and he stole from her while she was dying. She would have lived longer and definitely better if she'd had that money and I can never forgive him for that. Besides I need that money to live, as I told you. I'm trying to save my own life, now. It's too late for Myrna."

When their desserts came, and Barry had finished his second drink, he began to talk about what went wrong in New York. Elliot listened with disbelief as Barry described an F.B.I. agent bursting into the room he was renting, drawing a gun, and arresting him.

"I don't understand. Who called them?"

"I told you before. Kenneth called them, this hack writer former friend of mine who was storing a painting that I didn't take to Paris when I left New York three years ago. It's a Dufy watercolor—worth about eight to ten thousand. It used to hang above my mother's bed when we lived in Sutton Place. Do you remember it?"

"I remember."

"Basically he didn't want to give it up. His wife just had a kid and his career's going nowhere and he knows what the painting's worth, of course. So we had a fight on the phone and he threatened to throw the painting in the garbage, do you believe that?—the painting that used to hang above my mother's bed—and I yelled some things at him and he hung up. He wouldn't speak to me so I wrote him a letter."

"What did you say in the letter?"

"I guess I threatened him a little and the little prick whom I'd befriended and helped for years—and I saved his marriage, Elliot; he wouldn't be married much less a father if it weren't for me—this crooked little prick called the F.B.I. on me."

The story didn't end there. Other people were involved, another former friend who was storing Myrna's furniture, but by then Elliot's attention had begun to fade. An image of Irene, his dark-haired, brown-eyed wife, swooped over him suddenly like a great dark bird that seemed to carry him away. Irene often came to him like that when he least expected it and left him feeling a mix of yearning and rage and he'd begin reviewing for the thousandth time, perhaps, the sequence of events that led to their divorce and to his still being childless at his age despite all his plans and wishes to the contrary.

What did he have now to replace her with? For the last few months he'd been sleeping with Nickey, a real estate agent, who was very nice to him but it wasn't the same thing. His attention went back to Barry who was describing how heroic Megan, his legal aid attorney, had been in dealing with the F.B.I. mess. She kept him out of jail but the trade-off was he had to leave the country a week from now. A week might well not be enough time for him to get it done, but he felt Megan would be able to get him another extension.

"After this is all over, I think she'll have an affair with me, and she's gorgeous, Elliot, young and gorgeous."

None of this made any sense to Elliot, or even seemed like something that had really happened. He leaned back in his chair and closed his eyes for a few seconds. When he opened them again he decided he'd suspend judgment on whatever Barry said for the rest of the evening and just try to enjoy his company. There had been a lot of tension between them lately and Elliot found himself beginning to resent all the money he was spending on Barry. It was one thing to spend it on Irene, who had given him some great, irreplaceable years, but another to spend it on a man who didn't clean the toilet after himself, who probably was a compulsive liar, and yet whose approval Elliot was always trying to win. Wasn't that why they had always been so competitive with each other, and why their lifelong friendship had contained so many silent years? But he was judging again, thinking again. At the first opportunity he brought up the movies—something over which they'd always enjoyed disagreeing—and sure enough a pleasurable argument ensued about Ingmar Bergman and Stanley Kubrick. For the next hour they were their old selves again having another of their laughably interminable debates.

By the time they got home Elliot was feeling intoxicated from their conversation. He kept his phone call with Nickey short, and when he finally lay down to sleep, images of his past with Barry swirled through his mind. There were the two of them playing touch football on the playground where they went to grammar school in Brookline. There were he and Barry in Tanglewood excitedly discussing the girls from Canada they'd picked up at the concert and were going to go swimming with the next day. He saw them next as 18-year-olds in Myrna's living room in Brookline listening to Mahler's Resurrection Symphony, and in Myrna's Sutton Place apartment in their early thirties, reunited after not seeing each other in five years, Barry moving towards him with a drink in hand, saying, "I guess we're both a little nervous." And then, less than a year later, Barry's arm around his shoulder after Elliot's father died, Barry's sheer strength as he helped him move his boxes of manuscripts out of Elliot's Riverside Drive apartment to Elliot's new apartment in Astoria, Elliot seeing then in Barry's face, for a moment, the child he had played touch football with in so many schoolyard victories.

A routine established itself for the next five days. Elliot would write in the early morning before it got too hot. He had air conditioning in his room but he needed to pace while he was working and so used the white formica table in the kitchen and paced around the living room from time to time, secure that Barry wouldn't be disturbed. It was true that Elliot generally wrote in the morning but it was also true that since Barry arrived he felt he was writing with more energy and inventiveness.

After eating a bagel and reading the newspaper he took a shower, went through his mail, then worked on *The Glass Menagerie* production. Generally, two or three of the actors came to his apartment and, after walking around his "houseguest from Paris," still sound asleep on the living room futon, discussed or read through some scenes behind the closed door of his office.

It wasn't that his routine was really different in any substantial way than it was before Barry, rather that he was constantly aware of Barry— of the intense atmosphere between them and of Barry's constant desire to vent about the past and all the injustices he'd suffered. By night Elliot often felt the need to flee the apartment, and for a while began seeing Nickey more often than usual. When he was with her, however, his conversation was dominated by Barry's latest doings. At first, she laughed at his accounts of domestic life with his old, eccentric friend but soon she began to warn him.

"He's taking up all your time and energy, and money. If you don't watch it you'll become destitute too," she said, pointing an accusatory finger at him. "If I were you I'd give him a deadline by which time he has to leave, and a dollar limit you won't exceed on him, and be firm. Draw your line in the sand and don't let him cross it. It's plain as day he's manipulating you."

Barry's routine was very different and Elliot was mostly glad it was, as this gave him some sense of his former privacy for a few hours a day. After sleeping till 12:00 or 12:30, Barry would go out for his morning coffee at a European style cafe around the corner, where he insisted he did much of his thinking about his situation. "I'm thinking all the time, Elliot, much more than you realize. A lot of times when you think I'm sleeping, even when my eyes are closed, I'm doing some of my most intense thinking. There's so much on my mind I have to sort it out before I can move."

Generally Barry came back from the cafe around 3:00 or 3:30 then locked himself up in Elliot's office and used the phone for a couple of hours. Elliot tried to respect his privacy but as often as not he'd tiptoe out of his bedroom into the hallway and try to hear a few words.

Around five o'clock Barry had his aperitif—a glass of vodka and tonic—and would talk with Elliot about the day's events. Barry also stuck to his European habits when it came to dinner, which he "couldn't possibly eat" before 8:00 or 8:30, so they rarely ate together as Elliot was used to eating dinner at 6:00.

After dinner Barry would go to a bar "to nurse a drink; believe me, I know I can't afford more than one or two." It was at a local bar that he made friends with a young female bartender named Renee, or so he said. Naturally she was young and pretty and charming, Elliot thought to himself dismissively. On Wednesday night of that week Barry said he had a date with her. Elliot's own plans with Nickey fell through and he found himself alone in his air conditioned room with the TV on, intermittently thinking about Irene and wondering if he shouldn't call her, but more often thinking angrily about Barry. Where was the son of a bitch? Was his date real then? And how was he able to get all these young women and have a young lover like Arriane in Paris? French or American he conned them all, as if lying were the true international language and Barry was one of its masters. Elliot shook his head. So here he was alone while Barry was dating a woman in her twenties (young enough probably to be Nickey's daughter) with *his* money. He gripped the arms of his easy chair and gritted his teeth. It was getting later and later. When he finally heard the key turn he shut his door, turned the TV off in disgust, and tried to keep his eyes closed.

· · · · · · · · · ·

Everything changed the next day. When Elliot walked into his office to call Nickey, he saw Barry get up from the chair by the phone, his face white, his eyes stricken. "I didn't get the extension."

"What do you mean?" Elliot said, realizing in that moment that he hadn't been paying attention to Barry's legal situation lately because he no longer wanted to judge if it were true.

"I just got off the phone with Megan."

"Your legal aid person?"

"Yes, She said the prosecutor got a complaint from Kenneth, the worm who stole my painting."

"But you got the painting back."

"Yes, and I had to write a letter to get it, which is when he called the Feds on me."

"But I thought that was all settled."

"He claims I called him and threatened him a couple of nights ago.

The prosecutor believes it and that violates the terms of my probation, don't you see? I wasn't supposed to contact him."

"Not that it matters, but did you call him?"

"No, of course not. What reason would I have? I'd already gotten the painting back. I had other things on my mind like how to get the money that's owed me from my father and how to save my life."

He paced off a semicircle in front of the book cases, then stopped and looked directly into Elliot's eyes.

"So now I have two choices which really aren't choices at all. I can go to Paris with no money or place to live and just die, or go to jail here and die that way. Or somehow win the hearing and get the prosecutor to reverse herself and give me an extension again, which Megan says isn't likely. Elliot, if I lose the hearing they'll have me right there in court, don't you see? No, there's no way I'll let that happen, I'd rather kill myself than go to jail. We both know how I'll end up in jail."

"Would it do any good if I called Kenneth and tried to get him to drop the charges?"

"Would you? What do I have to lose?"

"O.K., I can do that."

"Remember, he's very angry and paranoid so you have to be careful how you talk to him."

For the next hour they discussed the best approach to use with Kenneth. There were a lot of things to consider. He was not only a hack writer, Barry said, but pretty much a failed hack writer, down on his luck, who was jealous of Barry because he was publishing serious books and had never compromised an iota in his work. Moreover, he and his wife had just had a baby and Kenneth was panicked about money, which was why he tried to hold onto the painting he'd been storing in the first place—he wanted to sell it. Barry said that Kenneth's anger came from his guilt at not helping him more and that he needed to be reminded that Barry had been a good friend for years and had played a crucial role in his getting married. Elliot listened, asking a question here and there, but by the time he was ready to make the call decided he was simply going to beg Kenneth to drop the charges.

While the phone rang Elliot reminded himself to keep his own emotions in check and to be as gentle and humble as possible. The first thing he had to do was to keep him on the phone. It wasn't going to be easy. As soon as he mentioned Barry's name, Kenneth started yelling. "What's your interest in this? Why are you calling me?"

Elliot took a breath. "My only interest is that I'm worried, really worried, that Barry may kill himself if he's forced to go back to Paris, and I'm simply calling you to beg you to consider dropping your charges against him."

"That fuck isn't going to kill himself! That fuck isn't going to die. He's like Freddie Krueger, he's indestructible. He's always threatening to kill himself—it's like his daily vitamin. Look, you understand that he threatened to kill me in writing, don't you? I'm a family man with a baby. We've been living in terror, double-bolting our door, jumping every time the phone rings. I want that phony fuck out of the country and that's just where he's going."

Elliot, speaking softly, said he was sorry Kenneth and his family had to go through that. That Barry was profoundly sorry, too, for writing the letter and that, of course, he would never follow through on anything like that. Barry was harmless and incapable of physical violence.

"What makes you such an expert on what Barry Rosenthal is capable of doing? What did you say your name was?"

"My name's Elliot. I've known Barry for over thirty years. We were best friends in grammar school and high school."

"Oh yeah? How come I never heard your name come up in all the years I talked with Barry? Where do you figure in the equation?"

Elliot swallowed hard and said nothing for a moment. He was stung that he'd mattered so little to Barry that he'd never been mentioned, even in passing, to Barry's latest New York friends.

"We had a falling out and hadn't spoken for a number of years."

"Until he needed you, right?"

"The point is I know about Barry's temper. He's yelled at me, he's even written me an abusive letter, but he's never, ever, gotten into a physical fight with me or any of our mutual friends. So let me reassure you that he never would have done anything like that with you. I understand the problem had something to do with a painting of his, some misunderstanding about it."

"He got mad at me when he called me from Paris and I couldn't find a place for him to stay in New York. The last time he stayed with me and my wife it was like staying with a five-year-old. He was filthy, disgusting."

"But he's got his painting back," Elliot interrupted. "So he has no reason to be angry at you. Are you sure it was him who called you?

"Does any other living creature have a voice like that?"

"How long did he talk? He says, of course, that he never called you."

"He's a compulsive liar and a delusional fuck. Believe me, it was long enough to tell. I don't need more than a sentence to tell with that crazy fuck. It was an invitation to step outside and settle things on the street, O.K.? Look, you may mean well but you're very naive. Barry's a total fraud. He's a pathetic tumor of a man and if I didn't have a child I would have met and fought him. Have you ever seen him with his mother? They acted like lovers. I wouldn't be surprised if they'd slept together all those years."

"Believe me, they never did," Elliot said.

"But there was some sick dynamic going on there, you can't deny it. And he's no writer either. He's never written anything, much less published anything. I checked him out once at Farrar, Straus—supposedly his American publisher—and they'd never heard of him. He can talk the talk, that's all.

"I know that he lies about his books and other things. I know all that. But I knew him when he really was writing and publishing back in his twenties. I read his articles in the *Voice*. I knew him when he was a brilliant and whole person. And he's still kind, still basically good, and so I'm begging you . . ."

But when the conversation ended a half hour later, Kenneth wouldn't relent.

· · · · · · · · ·

They entered a kind of nightmare space where the two of them paced around the apartment together. Elliot kept his answering machine on so he could concentrate better and didn't return Nickey's call. He stayed up almost as late as Barry that night, pacing and discussing the situation, but didn't sleep as long the next morning and finally woke Barry up earlier than usual.

Barry had wanted him to phone Kenneth again but Elliot said he'd seemed absolutely resolute. Then Barry said he wanted to send Kenneth a fax and Elliot yelled at him "Are you crazy? That would be violating your probation again. That's what got you into this mess in the first place. You're supposed to have no contact with him, no contact!"

Finally they decided that Elliot should speak to Megan, Barry's legal aid attorney, just to be sure Barry was clear about what his options were, and they both walked into the office while Elliot made the call. The news from Megan wasn't good. She pushed hard for Barry to obey the order and leave America in 36 hours. Did he have the means to buy a ticket to Paris? Elliot said he would buy Barry a ticket. Then there was really no reason for Barry not to go. If he went he'd avoid a hearing and possibly jail that way, and the court would look at his complying with their order as a good faith gesture which would help his chances of regaining his status in America down the road.

"I can't go back to Paris or I'll die," Barry said, while Elliot was still on the phone. "I have no money, no home, no way of making money. I'm over $10,000 in debt in my rent. I don't even have a visa. I won't make it, don't you see?"

"He says he won't go back to Paris, that he'll die there. What are his chances of winning at the hearing?"

Megan said it was hard to say. Would Elliot be willing to go to the hearing in New York and testify about Barry's character? Of course, Elliot said. The problem was, Megan said, that Barry had put his threats in writing and the prosecutor had copies of the letters. It wasn't that Kenneth wanted to punish Barry but he couldn't help regarding him as a threat to his family.

"But he's been here with me for almost two weeks and absolutely nothing's happened except this so-called phone call. He hasn't even left the state."

"Would you consider housing him for the duration of his extension, if he gets it, and guarantee that he won't leave Pennsylvania?"

"How long would that be?" Elliot said, looking over his shoulder at Barry and hoping that he somehow didn't know what was being discussed.

"No more than three weeks."

"That would be difficult. If I testify at the hearing, which of course I'll do, what do you think his chances are?"

Megan said it depended on the prosecutor, whom she didn't know very well but had heard was supposed to be a decent woman.

"And if he loses?"

"He'll be deported and possibly have to go to jail."

"Christ! Would it do any good if I spoke to this prosecutor on the phone, stressing how harmless Barry is, how he really does have prospects of getting the money he needs to live in Paris—that kind of thing?"

"It couldn't hurt if you're willing to do it. Let me call her first and see how she feels about it."

An hour later Megan called back and told Elliot that the prosecutor seemed like a reasonable woman and that if he were willing to call her in the next ten minutes before she left work it was certainly worth a try. There was no time to be nervous or even self-conscious. He asked to be alone, but Barry wouldn't hear of it. It was his fate that was being decided, and he simply had to be there. Finally they compromised; Barry would be in the room, available to give suggestions or information via written notes, but would remain quiet.

Almost from the beginning, Elliot felt the call wouldn't go well. He pretty much read the opening statement he'd written in five frantic minutes about his own background and his relationship with Barry, but Ms. Donovsky heard it without comment. Then she began to barrage him with arguments of her own. She had the victims' rights to consider. She was dealing with frightened people, a frightened family. If she made the wrong decision and something happened, it was on her head, her conscience. Elliot said again that Barry was harmless, merely had a child's quick temper. Donovsky countered with the letters and answering machine tape from Barry, hard evidence in her possession that she couldn't ignore. It was an incredibly stupid thing for Barry to have done, Elliot agreed. It was worse than that; it was a federal crime to threaten someone's life in writing, Donovsky said.

That was how it went (as Barry paced the room): a downward spiral into a horrible darkness, a defeat or dismissal for every point he made. Finally he heard himself pleading for Barry, saying he was frightened for his life, and only then after 45 minutes did she ask him the same question that Megan had asked about housing Barry and keeping him out of New York *if* she granted him an extension. "Until when?" Elliot asked softly.

"No later than August first—three weeks from now," Donovsky said. Would he sign an affidavit guaranteeing this?

"Yes" Elliot said. Then he was suddenly off the phone, telling Barry "You got the extension," and something broke in Barry's face as if it had collapsed.

He sobbed once, then squeezed Elliot's hand as hard as it had ever been squeezed, and softly said, "Thank you."

Elliot felt dazzled, felt an ecstasy he knew he could never explain to anyone. He had done something important in his life, something that mattered for someone he cared about, and it had all been worth it. Suddenly his own life, not just Barry's, had been redeemed for a moment and crowned with meaning.

* * * * * * * * *

The routines continued in the following days, complete with their irritations and tensions and occasional moments of sharp pleasure, as when Barry would tell an especially amusing anecdote about Gore Vidal or Michel Foucault, though Elliot never knew if they were true or the product of Barry's fecund imagination. On the truth issue he had come to some conclusions. All the bad things, or certainly most of them, that Barry said had happened to him were true—time had proven that. It was the literary and sexual triumphs that Barry needed to counteract his tragedies which were probably all made up. It was with them that Barry had trouble or simply didn't want to separate fantasy or wild hope from reality. Unfortunately, that tendency extended to his prospects for getting money. Barry was not only trying to get his one-hundred-twenty thousand from his father, who'd already rejected him, and from personal friends (all in vain, of course) but was also spending an astronomical amount of Elliot's money calling and faxing independent businessmen and speculators—offering them twice their money back against the million dollars he claimed he would receive for his next book about corruption and scandal in the East Hampton police department. The book, the super-agent, the contract didn't exist, at least not objectively. Elliot was sure of that. "What I wonder," he said to Nickey while they were talking in bed in her apartment, "is does he know he's lying when he says these things to people, or at this point does he actually believe it?"

"What I wonder about is when are you going to stop worrying about this guy and get your own life back. He's eating you alive."

Was Barry eating him alive? Nickey's words echoed in his mind later like a mantra. There were times, as when he was sponging up last evening's wine stains or sweeping Barry's latest trail of crumbs, that he felt an anger surging up in him, felt her words to be true. But there were other times, when Barry was at a cafe or at a bar at night or even sometimes when the conversation was dragging with Nickey, when Elliot felt his absence keenly. Moreover, there were times within those times when Elliot not only missed Barry but felt a void when he was gone as if part of his own personality were missing. Was his life without Barry so dull that there was nothing to replace him with? His marriage had not been dull, as he thought of Irene with a sudden stab of pain, but everything with her was destroyed and lost as if he'd had to experience an equal amount of anguish to make up for the intense joy he'd once had with her. Though he mostly complained about Barry to Nickey, or whoever else would listen, he had to acknowledge that even now there was nothing quite as exhilarating as arguing with him about literature or music, nothing that pleased him in quite the same way as Barry praising one of his plays or articles.

Meanwhile, in a tense and furious kind of counterpoint, there was his anger and anxiety about the money it was costing to feed Barry and pay for his calls, there was the ongoing distrust and exasperation as one after another of Barry's schemes to raise money fell through—a result that was totally predictable to Elliot but was experienced each time as a fresh horror by Barry.

As Barry's days in Philadelphia dwindled, Elliot's anxiety that Barry would ultimately double-cross him increased. He had already admitted the other night that he had made the telephone call to Kenneth while he was drunk. The fear that Barry would violate the prosecutor's agreement and get him in trouble with the F.B.I. persistently haunted him and ultimately tipped the scales in favor of his wanting Barry to leave, made him finally call the travel agency when he saw that Barry was stalling and buy him a non-refundable ticket to Paris. Barry's hand shook a little as he took the ticket.

Two days later Barry was sitting in the brown reclining chair drinking a vodka, staring blankly in front of himself.

"Don't you think you should start to pack?" Elliot said. "The train to the airport leaves at ten tomorrow morning."

"I'll pack," Barry said with an ironic smile. "But I can't promise you about going to Paris."

"What do you mean you can't promise? What are you talking about?" Barry sat up, suddenly charged with energy.

"No matter how intelligent and empathetic you are, and you are both, and no matter how well you know me—and since Myrna died you probably know me better than anyone in the world—you still can't be inside my head, you still can't really understand my situation and why I have to do what I have to. And you don't know what's facing me in Paris. But I do."

"I know what's facing you here. The United States Government is ordering you out of the country tomorrow. There are no more extensions; the prosecutor was absolutely clear about that."

"I think they realize they made a mistake, by now. I think the F.B.I. realizes they have more important people to worry about than me."

"You can't take that chance. If they find you they'll put you in jail," Elliot said, turning around so that he faced Barry, who was now leaning forward intently in his chair, a few feet in front of him, like a jockey.

"I may have to. I'm turning it over in my mind."

"What the fuck is there to turn over? You have no money, no prospects of getting any money."

"You don't know that. I can have a meeting with Ted Turner in a matter of days, the same with Jack Nicholson. In my mind I still think I can get it done. In my mind . . ."

"Fuck your mind, it's full of delusions . . . about this. Your father doesn't have it, you can't get it from the art dealer—all the people you've sent faxes to, the guy from Smith Barney, they've all said 'no'—there's no one left, but you. You've got to get a job, Barry, that's what you've got to do, any job, tutoring, translating something where you can set your own hours, and go back to your apartment in Paris or to Arriane. Working is, finally, how everyone else makes money and you've got to do it too."

"The power's off in my apartment. Remember I'm over $10,000 in debt on my rent. They may have locked up my apartment. As for getting a job, it's not that simple. I don't even have a visa."

"I don't understand about that. I don't understand what you were thinking while your rent was accumulating, if you didn't think you could work."

"Elliot, I wasn't well. I was in trauma because of my mother. I still don't completely believe she's dead, I've been through things you can't conceive of. I have no right to be alive."

"The point is if you don't go back tomorrow you're a wanted man with no money or place to stay. I mean, you can't stay here. Here is the first place they'd look."

"Don't worry, you won't get in trouble. I'd never let that happen to you. I'll leave here tomorrow and you'll have fulfilled your promise to the feds, capiche? You won't have to know where I'm going or what I'm doing. I won't even tell you, O.K.?"

"Why can't you stay at Arriane's?"

"Did I show you her latest letter?" Barry said with a smile, getting up from the chair and removing the letter from a folder of correspondence that lay half on the radiator, half on the window sill.

"You translated it to me."

"No, no, this is a new one she just sent, she wrote it in English."

"Barry, there's no time for this. Why can't you stay with her? Let her carry you for a while."

"She's only twenty-four. I don't know how mature she is, how attracted to her I really am. I've only known her for a few months—it wouldn't be fair to either of us. But I'm still turning it over in my mind. I haven't decided on anything definite yet. But whatever, I won't compromise you. You'll never know what I decide and if I can't go on you'll get my paintings."

"I don't want your paintings."

"It's already in my will. I've sent a copy to Arriane and one to Megan."

A half hour later Elliot stopped arguing and went to his room to try to sleep. It wouldn't get any better than this. He would have to let him go without asking where and try to believe he was going to Paris. He could not let him stay any longer even if he wanted to. It was against the law and so Barry simply had to leave in this profoundly unsatisfying way.

He woke Barry up early, and, as he expected, he hadn't finished packing. While Barry showered, Elliot walked around the living room, stopping to look through Barry's bags a few times to be sure he hadn't taken any of his favorite shirts which he'd been intermittently lending him. He hadn't, and Elliot felt slightly ashamed for checking.

Once out of the shower Barry began obsessively checking things. It seemed impossible for him to do anything in a non-melodramatic way, or before the last minute. Finally, on the street corner they got a cab while there was still theoretically enough time for Barry to catch the plane.

"Write me from Paris," Elliot said, putting two hundred dollars into Barry's hand. "Don't contact me till you've gotten there, O.K.?"

"O.K.," Barry said with a strange smile. "Don't worry, I'm doing what I have to do, capiche? And thanks a million, thanks for everything. There are no words." Then without turning his head to wave goodbye, and sitting up unusually rigid like a mummy in the back seat, Barry rode away in the cab.

He's not going to Paris, he would have told me if he were, Elliot thought, once back in his living room. Later, as he reviewed the morning he thought there was something ominous about Barry's last words. He was supposed to see Nickey that night for a celebratory date but an hour later called her to cancel, saying his stomach was bothering him.

"Well, thank God, he's gone at last," Nickey said. "Now do me a favor and air out your apartment. Open all your windows and, once you feel better, wash and disinfect everything. I don't want to smell him when I'm in your bed . . . What's the matter? You sound sad," she said a minute later. "You did nothing but complain about him when he was there. He made your life a living hell. Don't tell me you miss him."

"I'm worried about him that's all."

"You act like he's your child."

"Irene wouldn't have a baby with me. Maybe I needed someone to take care of," he said with a little laugh.

When he got off the phone he was surprised that his stomach really did hurt. He took an Ativan and tried to sleep.

In the morning when the actors from *The Glass Menagerie* came over, he felt better for a while. They'd been used to quietly filing past Barry's sleeping body en route to Elliot's office to rehearse. This time, when they saw the suddenly empty living room, one of them said "Where's your house guest?"

"The man who came to dinner has finally gone," Elliot said.

The actors laughed a little nervously but were certainly glad to rehearse in the much more spacious living room. After they'd left, the silence in his apartment was oppressive, as if it were attacking him. He tried turning on the radio, then listening to records, but the music made things worse. He began compiling the notes and messages, left in various parts of the apartment, that Barry had written to him to update him on his financial and emotional condition. He read them a couple of times, then put them in a cabinet in his kitchen. He decided he would take a walk before it got too hot, perhaps around Rittenhouse Square, when something caught his eye. On the floor, half hidden by the radiator, was the letter Arianne had written in English that Barry had wanted to read to him the night before he left. It was a two-page letter written in flowing blue ink full of exclamation points—a curious mix of romantic enthusiasm, cosmic bitterness, and youthful French intellectualism. But her passion and tenderness, her offer to help him "if you only tell me what to do," were unmistakable. He thought of Irene and wished he had written her such a letter. Why had he held himself back when it might have made a difference? One line in the letter particularly moved him. "When I am alone in my apartment, where just a little while ago we were together, I can feel, like something palpable, your dignity, your silence, the magnificent mass of your dreams."

Was this Barry the compulsive liar, the slob, the "tumor of a man," as Kenneth had called him. Yes, Barry did have not only magnificent dreams but real dignity and goodness as well. It was the same man; the slob and the saint were one. How could he have let Barry leave without knowing where he was going, without saying that he could call him, without being sure if he would live or die.

Tears filled his eyes, and when he closed them he felt dizzy and went to his room to lie down.

The next morning he woke up with a sore throat and a fever. He called Megan to see if she had any news from Barry but she said she hadn't heard anything. Hadn't he gone to Paris? He called Arriane. He tried her periodically for three hours but there was no answer. Perhaps she was away on vacation or with her theater troupe. Perhaps she was on her way to meet Barry, or to try to save him.

He went back to his room, to his television and fever. Nickey called and offered to come over and help him but he said he needed to be alone.

That night he dreamed he was swimming with Barry in very blue water. Suddenly he heard Barry call out to him for help, signaling frantically as he went underwater. Elliot dove and looked around at the strange fish and plants operating with their own rules, which he didn't understand, in a world he'd never seen before, which frightened him. He wanted to help Barry but felt paralyzed. Then he began to yell until he woke up with a start.

He was perspiring and his throat hurt. He took an Ativan and two Tylenols and slept uneasily for the next few hours.

The next day he tried reasoning with himself more aggressively. He had gone the extra mile with Barry—he'd gone the extra ten miles—so there was no reason to feel guilty. He'd housed and fed him for over a month, let him make hundreds of dollars of phone calls, signed an affidavit and assumed legal responsibility for him, cleaned up his errant piss and wine and unflushed shit, neglected his own work and girlfriend, given him clothes, time, energy and advice, bought him a ticket to Paris, spent nearly two thousand dollars on him, but because of the way Barry manipulated him he was feeling awful simply because Barry had pigheadedly refused to fly back, had preferred to break the law and be a fugitive than to go back to Paris. What kind of person was he? What kind of friend was that? For him to feel guilt was ridiculous. He didn't feel guilty, in fact, but he did feel awful, and every time the phone rang he was angry when it wasn't Barry, and even exploded at Nickey, who was probably ready to dump him by now.

By Saturday morning he'd begun to give up. If Barry were alive in America he would have called by now. Though he said he'd spent a night on the street when he first came to New York, he couldn't spend four, could he? When the phone rang in the middle of the afternoon he no longer raced to answer, but picked up on the fourth ring.

"Elliot, it's Barry. I'm at the Rittenhouse Cafe around the corner. I'm in a desperate situation. Can I stay with you for a few days?"

For a moment he felt suffused with joy but it quickly turned to anger.

"What are you doing here? You're supposed to be out of the country."

"You knew I wasn't going back, that I couldn't go back. I was staying with Renee, the bartender, but she's having a crisis in her family and I can't stay there any more. Elliot, I had no choice."

"I told you not to call me till you were in Paris. How do you have the balls to assume I'll put you up? I'd be harboring a fugitive from the F.B.I. It's against the law, goddamn it!"

"I got an extension. Megan got it for me."

"That's a lie!" Elliot screamed. "I called her two days ago and she hadn't even heard from you."

"Did you speak to her yesterday? She worked something out with the prosecutor Friday afternoon, provided I stay with you."

"You're manipulating me, you're lying."

"I can't believe you don't trust me on this. You can call her on Monday and she'll tell you herself."

"You lied to me about Kenneth."

"I had no choice then. I said one line to him when I was drunk. Elliot, I'm fighting for my life, please . . ."

He continued talking but Elliot no longer listened to him. Instead he was remembering the look in Barry's eyes as he squeezed his hand that day in the office when he won his extension, then the two of them listening to Mahler's Second Symphony in Myrna's living room in Brookline twenty-five years ago, tears in their eyes from the powerful music. A few minutes later Elliot walked into the cafe and tapped Barry on the shoulder. "Come on, let's go."

Barry got up from his table and looked away from him.

"I'm sorry I yelled at you," Elliot said, extending his hand. Barry shook it and Elliot half embraced him with his other arm.

"It's all right now. You can stay another week and we'll both talk to Megan on Monday, O.K.? I can take a little chance till then."

BODYSURFING

There was a rustling, then Lee saw it, fat and gray and big-eyed with an orange crown, as it slid across the path. They were going to have the last laugh—the iguanas—that was for sure. There were so many of them, Costa Rica was going to be their world some day. The path ended and the boogie board banged against his knee. He swore out loud as he began walking down the road. It was madness, sheer madness, to have rented the board. He knew that within two minutes; he knew that when he reached the first wave. There was the wave and his body and nothing ever should come between them, that alone should be pure. Sheer lunacy to think otherwise. He looked at it—baby blue with a dangling wrist strap like an umbilical cord, this boogie board with its silly name—it was idiocy in its purest form to let it ruin his rides, to let it bang about in the wind and hit his knee. Why had he done it, why? It was because he'd remembered his wife saying they were so much fun. Years ago she'd said that; he had a distant memory of it. It was that and the surfboard morons who were taking over the ocean, crowding him out of his space. He'd let them intimidate him, let them infantilize him into thinking he should maybe get some kind of board of his own, so when he left the beach and saw it in the store he'd rented it on an impulse.

It was the same store that was in front of him now. The Palm Store, a combination travel agency and gift shop run by a good-looking man and his wife with a yellow-haired kid who didn't look like either of them, certainly not the man. So he would return it now, eleven minutes after he took it. Of course he wouldn't ask for his money back. He would take responsibility. They would wonder why, perhaps ask him why, but he wouldn't let himself worry about it. He was about to lose his job in two weeks, about to be transferred to a lower job in the bank in a different city, to be screwed over like that at his age, and with his mother at death's door, too. No, he wasn't going to worry about returning a boogie board to a store that looked like it was made out of cards (as every other store in Tamarindo did), with its pathetically corny painting of a sun sinking below the waves, a store that rented surfboards and goggles and boogie boards and tickets for turtle tours!

He went inside the Palm Store. A tall attractive blond man, a surfboardoron, perhaps two inches taller than he was, perhaps a dozen years younger, perhaps with fourteen better-defined muscles than he had, had finished talking to the owner and was fingering a surfboard as Lee placed the boogie board beside it. He is going to ask me how I liked the boogie board, Lee thought. He is going to try to have a conversation with me. The blond man turned toward Lee. He is from California, Lee thought.

"How did it ride?" the blonde man said.

"How did it ride? It didn't ride at all. I didn't have any use for it."

"Surf too strong today?"

"Board too superfluous today, or any day."

"O.K. I hear you."

Lee was struck by how straight the surfer's teeth were, which perhaps accounted for the extraordinary hang time of his smile.

"I don't like anything to come between me and the wave, me and the water. I think that relationship ought to stay pure. Today I violated that relationship, I'm sorry to say. Today I let myself be conquered by a product and I corrupted that relationship."

The blond man's smile vanished and Lee felt vindicated.

"I don't think I get what you mean."

"These boards," Lee said, indicating the blond man's surfboard with his gesture, "they're just another way people've found to make money off the water. They're about buying and selling, that's all."

The blond man showed a second smile, a quizzical but still friendly one. "I guess I don't see it that way," he said.

"Really? How do you see it, then?"

"They're just a piece of equipment for a sport. They're just a means to an end. Like you can't play baseball without a bat or football without a ball, can you?"

Lee felt an adrenalin rush. Apparently the man really wanted to discuss this. "There was a time when you could play sports without buying things," Lee said. "To me the more a sport costs the less its value. The more it's about buying these accessories, the more of a fetish it becomes instead of a sport. By the way, I hope I didn't desecrate the flag, so to speak, with my remarks about surfboards. I know you guys get sensitive about that."

"No, man. I don't mind. I just never met anyone who thinks like you. It's kind of interesting, really."

Lee felt flattered in spite of himself. Ridiculous to feel that in this situation, though he did for a moment, and thought he should soften himself. Besides he was beginning to get an idea and he needed time to figure it all out. Just before he spoke he made a point of looking at the surfer's eyes.

"And by the way, I know whereof I speak," Lee said. "I'm a banker. You can't be much more of a whore than that. My whole life is buying and selling. I'm in middle management at Citibank. Need I say more? Or I soon will be. I was actually at a somewhat higher level of management but that's like bragging about being in a higher circle of hell, isn't it? But at least on my vacation I want to stay pure when I'm in the water. I said to my secretary, 'I don't care what kind of hotel you get me (and she got me Le Jardin del Eden, the most expensive one in Tamarindo) but I insist on big, world-class waves. I want you to research that for me.' Well, the waves here are certainly world class and they deserve the best from me."

Lee looked closely at the man, who in turn appeared to be concentrating intensely on what Lee said. "So, I'm on my way now, I'm going to have my twilight drink, and again, I hope I haven't offended you at all."

"No way. I enjoyed talking with you. You're the first American I've spoken to in three days. I don't speak Spanish so I've practically been talking to myself since I've been here."

Lee looked at him closely once more, wondering if he were gay or just needy, or perhaps one of those friendly, new age types. He had decided something important, something definitive in the waves yesterday but this young man might make it even better. Besides he was a surfer and that would make him the cherry on the sundae and his possible gayness would never enter into it.

"I've enjoyed it too," Lee said. "Hey, you know the restaurant, Zully-mar?"

"Sure."

"That's where I'm going for my drink. Why don't you join me and have one on the bank."

The blond man laughed. "Sure. My name's Andy," he said, extending his hand.

"I'm Lee Bank or should I say Le Bank, and we all know what shape banks are in."

Lee turned and walked out of the store and Andy followed after him, still laughing.

"Is Bank really your last name?"

"I'm sometimes known as Lee Bastard, or when I'm in Paris as Le Bastard. But we are far from Paris now, aren't we?"

Lee looked straight ahead as they walked down the dirt road and seemed unaware that Andy was walking beside him. It was not much of a road, Lee thought, full of holes and rocks and puddles, so they could have, should have left it alone and not put up so many toy-like stores. Laughable really how small they were—the little shack that probably doubled as someone's home—with the giant sign saying "Nachos and Ice Cream," a sign that was half as big as the shack. Pathetic really, the hut beside it—called Jungle Bus—that advertised "Killer Burguer and mun-chies." If the puddle on the road in front of it rose a couple of inches, it could swallow the Jungle Bus.

Zullymar was on the other side of the road, facing the Jungle Bus on one side and the beach on the other. It was a big (by Tamarindo stan-dards) open-air restaurant and bar filled with surfers, the same crowd that forced him off his path two days in a row in the water and actually made him yearn for a lifeguard to patrol things. A wall mural that clashed with the red floor depicted a pink pelican, circling over some anchored boats and a small island beyond that—the approximate scene outside. Across the street at another bar, a man was playing the marimba with two little boys.

Lee and Andy sat down at a table facing the water and looked briefly at the half-filled room. As soon as they focused on each other Lee said, "You'll want a beer, won't you? Isn't that the drink you guys favor?" He had a tight, semisarcastic smile and Andy smiled back.

"What do you mean?"

"You surfers, you surf wizards. You don't want to drink anything too hard, anything that might put you at risk when you go out on your boards again."

"I'm done surfing for the day and I drink lots of things. No routine."

"Fine. Dos mai tais," Lee said to the waiter.

The incredulous smile reappeared on Andy's face. Lee was going to say something to try to get rid of it but Andy spoke first.

"You've got some negative feelings toward surfers, don't you?"

Lee shrugged.

"What did they do to you man?" Andy said, half-laughing, his hand absently caressing his board for a moment, Lee noticed, as if he really thought the goddamn thing was alive. "Did they run into you once or something?"

"No, that would never happen, though they have crowded me out more than once here in Tamarindo, kept me from where I wanted to go, but believe me I stick to my own path. I don't mingle. I am not only on a different path from them, I'm in a different world."

"But what's so different about your world?"

"Night and day, Andy, night and day."

"Why, what do you do? You bodysurf, right? I respect that. So I get up on a board and you bodysurf. Have you ever surfed?"

"I do surf."

"I mean with a board."

"Years ago when I was actually young."

"So what do you have against it?"

The drinks came. Andy took a big swallow while Lee let his sit.

"It's about buying and selling again. Kids see it on TV in ads and think 'that's it.' Then they make movies about it and create a surfing tour and sell all this equipment, all these fetishes, and the young guys think if I do this I'll be a man, if I do this I'll get some first-class pussy. It will all happen if I can just buy the right board."

Andy was laughing now. He was not an easy man to offend, Lee concluded, as he sipped his drink.

"I'm not agreeing with you, by the way," Andy said. "I just think what you're saying is funny and interesting in a way."

"Of course you think that surfboarding is the greater sport, the greater challenge, don't you? After all, you stand up, you are Homo Erectus, whereas I am still on all fours. You go out further to sea whereas I am nearer the shore. You walk on water like Jesus Christ whereas I only ride with it like a fish. And then when gravity must eventually bring you down you take the deeper, more heroic fall. You think all those things, don't you?"

"I just enjoy surfing. I haven't thought it out like that really. And like I say, I respect what you do."

"I wonder if you know what I do. Because there are a number of body-surfers out there—it isn't just me—and very few of them know when or how to jump, and once they do jump how to go with the wave. They almost always start too late."

"I probably wouldn't know man—isn't that the way it is with everything? We don't really understand the other person's thing or point of view."

"Dos mai tais," Lee said, catching the waiter's attention, although he had not yet made significant progress on his first drink.

"So, now tell me your story, Andy. What brings you to glorious Tamarindo?"

Andy looked flustered, ran his fingers twice through his longish blond hair. He could be Kato Kaelin's younger brother, Lee thought.

"I just came here to surf."

"From whence did you come, then?"

"Santa Cruz, in California."

Lee smiled tightly again. "This is your vacation then. You came to Tamarindo directly on your vacation?"

"Not exactly. I was in Monteverde first. I went to Costa Rica directly but I went to Monteverde first, you know, in the mountains.

"Then you are a mountain man, too."

Andy lowered his head a little. Lee couldn't tell if he were burying his smile or giving birth to a new one. In Tamarindo smiles were the iguanas on every surfer's face. Lee distrusted smiles in general because he had discovered that if you believed in them a time would come when that belief would hurt you. He remembered he had once been very moved by his wife's smile.

"So how were the mountains?" he finally said.

"Some bad stuff happened there so I came here earlier than I expected."

"I'm sorry to learn that. What exactly was the bad stuff?"

The waiters came with the new drinks and Andy took a big swallow as the waiter took his first glass, while Lee carefully placed his second glass next to his first (which was still three quarters full) as if he were positioning two bowling pins.

"The woman I was with went bad on me. She met a dude on the tour we took in the cloud forest. He was older than me, around your age I guess, and he had a lot more money than me, you know. I was never very good at making money. I just help run a little Xerox store. But this rich guy was a businessman, a big businessman, though he was in the same hotel as us, only he was in some luxury suite. Anyway, she told me she was sorry; she said she didn't plan it that way, that it was a one-in-a-million thing but she thought he was the man for her and she was going to go with him for the rest of her vacation and beyond. So . . ."

"So what could you do?"

"Just got drunk. Woke up alone the next morning and got in my Suzuki and came down here 'cause they said this was where the surf was, and they didn't lie about that. The last couple of days I took it out on the waves, six, seven hours a day, and just flushed that bitch right out. It hurt though, I'll tell you. So when you talk about money corrupting things, I really hear you."

"And when you talk about women being bitches, I hear you. I lost my sense of smell from a woman once."

"How'd that happen?" Andy's incredulous smile had snuck back, Lee noted, as if it were taking a curtain call.

"I discovered my female friend had cheated on me and I got extremely ill in an odd way. I developed a sinus condition that's never really gone away. I think it was my ex-wife who did me wrong, though it might have been someone else before her. Over the years people tend to blur together, don't they? Anyway, I have very little to do with women now. The only woman in my life besides Mother Sea is my secretary and she's far too valuable to bother having sex with. I am completely dependent on her. It was she who arranged this trip for me. Of course I'll lose her when I'm transferred to my next job but that's the way it is with women—we always lose them. They were put here on earth so we would know what losing is. Even when we have them we lose them—did you ever think about that?"

"What do you mean?"

"We watch them lose their looks, their charm, their ability to have children, their sex. We lose our mothers, too, and then our wives become our mothers and we lose them again. We lose our mothers a second time."

"But men age too," Andy said.

"But we don't notice it as much since we don't desire men, do we? Anyway, you don't have to worry about all this now. It'll be years before you'll have to realize this."

"I realize it; I realize some of it now."

"Then you might consider giving them up as I have. You can get a greater high than the orgasm from bodysurfing, at least you can the way I bodysurf."

Andy looked away morosely. Lee waited a minute. There was a rustling sound in the restaurant as if the waiters were really iguanas. Lee couldn't stand hearing it so he spoke.

"Thinking about her?" he said.

"Yeah."

"How long were you two an item?"

"Just a couple of months but . . ."

"Impact can be made in a couple of months. Impact can be made in a minute if we allow it to happen. I understand."

"Yeah, I thought this one would work out. I had hopes . . ."

"Ah hopes," Lee said, gesturing vaguely toward the sea. "Listen, I have an idea for you, a proposal to make to you. It does not involve hope, but something better. It involves a challenge."

"Go on."

"Something very special happened to me yesterday. Do you know that inlet that separates our beach from the other one, the one that goes straight to the mountains?"

"Yes."

"Have you ever been on that other beach?"

"No. No one surfs over there so I just assumed there wasn't much there."

"That's precisely the point. The beach goes on for miles but because there's no access from the road, because there is a thick jungle of trees to walk through and no other way to reach it unless you swim across the inlet, there is almost no one there. Well, yesterday I swam across that inlet. It was sunset, a little earlier than now, and the swim wasn't easy but I found the beach deserted and astonishingly beautiful. There were no footprints on the sand, just the swerving lines of hermit crabs and twisted branches from trees. I don't think there were even any butterflies; it wasn't civilized enough for them. It was like being on the moon or on a new planet. The waves were enormous and there was no one around to get in my way. My path was totally clear. Why don't you go there with me now and bodysurf with me? Leave your board at your hotel room and just go there with me now. I know you've only known me thirty minutes or whatever it's been. I know it's getting dark and it's a little dangerous."

"It's not that dangerous. I could do that."

"Fine, marvelous. Here, why don't you have my other drink, I haven't touched it, and I'll finish my first one and then we'll go out together and meet the waves with our bodies alone. I promise you it will be extraordinary."

"Yeah, O.K.," Andy said, looking Lee straight in the eye. "I'll go with you. I'm open to it."

They finished their drinks quickly and Lee paid the bill. The moment he put the money in the waiter's hand he saw the sun slip below the water. Some people were watching it in the restaurant and beyond them others watched from the beach. It was an understandable ritual, Lee thought. It had been advertised, like a Citibank card, and people needed to see the promise delivered. In her condominium in Florida, his mother was probably watching it, too, from her wheelchair, perhaps with one of her nurses. She more than anyone believed in advertised beauty. All her life she believed in Jackie Kennedy and Marilyn Monroe and Marlon Brando and Holiday Inns and sunsets. It would not do any good to tell her the deeper beauty came after the sunset, came with the night when the whole world slid below water. She had never listened to him. They should have switched positions. She should have worked for Citibank and he should have been the cripple. He might have done well in a chair . . .

There were only occasional street lamps outside but he could see the night was thick with butterflies. They were not talking now, so he could hear another iguana slide past in front of him. Then he decided it wouldn't have mattered if they were talking—he would have heard it anyway. In Tamarindo every sound on earth was an iguana; you could only escape them in the water.

"There's your hotel," Lee said, pointing to the Diria, barely bigger than the travel agency it seemed. "Why don't you drop your board off here, you won't be needing it. It'll only get in the way."

"O.K.," Andy said softly. He walked off in the dark and Lee waited in the road, thinking he should have told him 'go put your dick away there too. That's what your board really is. You won't be needing it where we're going. There aren't any dicks in the ocean, not in the night ocean.'"

Andy came back. Lee had never really considered that he wouldn't.

"Let's go," Lee said. There were about fifty yards of road before they reached the path that led to the beach. The deep orange of the sky had passed. It was now a dark purple and silver, tinged with spots of fading pink. There were not many people on the beach and most of them were leaving. Except for the white of the waves, the ocean was dark.

"It gets dark quickly," Andy said.

"Drops like a plank," Lee said. He is very young, Lee thought, and his fear is showing. Lee thought of himself as a thousand years old. This will be good for him. He needs to put on a hundred years. Then he didn't think about him anymore.

They walked the length of the beach toward the inlet. Andy was talking about the girl who had dumped him, whose name was Dawn.

"Forget the girl," Lee said. "Drown her in the ocean."

When they reached the inlet the sky was nearly black. There were lots of stars out and three quarters of a moon.

"I was hoping it would be low tide so we could walk across," Andy said.

"We can swim it," Lee said. He threw the towel he'd been carrying into the sky and the black swallowed it.

"What did you just do?"

"I threw my towel away. I won't be needing it. It's a hotel towel."

"Yeah, you told me about your hotel. Very impressive. It's supposed to be the best hotel in Tamarindo." There was sarcasm, even a trace of contempt, in Andy's voice that stung Lee for a second.

"The hotel can drop dead," Lee said as he walked into the water. He was surprised again by how wide the inlet was but he didn't feel tired this time while he was swimming. He could hear Andy breathing heavily, almost gasping, as he swam beside him and thought for a moment that he shouldn't have let him drink three mai tais.

"Stop racing," he said, nearly yelling. "Stop trying to beat me. It's not a race. You have to pace yourself."

Andy slowed down the rest of the way. When they reached the shore of the deserted beach there were only a few slivers of sky that weren't black.

"I wish it were lighter, man." Andy said.

"Why?"

"I can't see things you said would be here. I can't see the things you promised."

"Yes, you can. Look harder."

"I can barely see in front of myself."

"I can look at anything and see the beauty in it. Especially the dark."

"Tell me what I was supposed to see here again, and walk slower, will you? I can barely keep up with you."

"Twisted tree branches and hermit crab lines," Lee said.

Lee walked briskly, saying nothing for the next few minutes. Andy ran after him, stumbling occasionally, trying to keep up with him or at least keep him in sight, feeling like he did when he was a child trying to keep up with his father's longer, relentless stride.

"Come on, we're going in the water. It's time to face the black water now."

Lee walked toward the ocean in fast, imperious strides like a fixated scoutmaster, Andy thought.

"Slow down, will you, why are you racing?" Andy said, and then repeated himself, yelling this time because the ocean was so loud he felt he wasn't being heard.

Lee kept walking into the water without changing speed, the big blustery businessman from the fancy hotel who had to know it all, who had to take what he wanted when he wanted it. Why had he listened to him, why had he come with him to this crazy beach. He was chasing after him in the water now while his legs felt like rubber. The water was up to his knees and he knew something was wrong, had known it for some time.

"Lee," he yelled. "Lee. Lee Bastard."

A few seconds before he'd seen him fifteen yards ahead propelling himself forward, not even ducking for the waves but somehow willing himself forward like a man walking into a wall, into the earth, until the water covered him. Andy heard himself scream. It might have been "Lee," it might have been "Help." His legs wouldn't move at first and when they could he knew he wouldn't move them because he'd already known Lee wanted to be witnessed while he disappeared by a sucker like Andy, just as Dawn had, and one of those humiliations was enough. Lee Legend gets back at a surfer. Lee Lemming. "Lee," he screamed. "Lee Bastard," knowing he would see and hear nothing now except the constant roar in the black and his own sickly voice boomeranging back at him like spit in the wind, because the bastard had wanted it this way.

THE TOWEL

Steven no longer complained about his mother, at least not as much as he used to. As the time for his semiannual visit approached, he even stopped referring to her as "the Sympathy Junkie," or "the Miser." Lying in bed the night before his flight to Florida, he told Cherise that the last few months had been the best stretch of time in their marriage. He said that that was why he was feeling so much more sympathy lately toward his mother. After all, she was an eighty-year-old widow with real physical problems and, in spite of everything, he did love her deeply.

The next afternoon, while the airport limousine drove down the last few streets that led to his mother's home in Seaport, he resolved not to lose his temper no matter how much she provoked him. He tipped the driver a dollar more than he normally would and rode up the elevator to his mother's penthouse condominium feeling confident and unusually cheerful.

She answered the door holding her cane tightly as he walked in with a smile and a hug for her. It took her an extraordinarily long time to walk to the part of the living room that best showed off the view. In the past he'd often thought she was moving much more slowly than she needed to get as much sympathy from him as possible. He remembered how many times, after the initial walk from the door, he'd seen her move at least twice as fast without even using her cane, but he wouldn't allow himself to think of that now. Instead he looked at the photographs of his father, alone and with his mother, or at the photographs of his brother Daniel that adorned the walls (where he'd always felt pictures of him were underrepresented) until she finally arrived at her reclining chair by the picture window. He sat down at her desk opposite her, still looking around for an additional photograph of himself he might have missed.

"Let me look at you. I haven't seen you for a year," she said.

"It hasn't been a year. I visited you last Thanksgiving."

"Really? Well, eight months you've stayed away then instead of twelve—isn't that long enough? You look good, Stevie. You look better than you did last year."

He wanted to tell her about how well things were going now in his career and with Cherise, but before he could she said, "Here's a new post-card from Danny." She was waving it in the air as if it were a winning lottery ticket.

Then she put her glasses on and, holding the postcard up to the window, began reading it loudly. Steven only half listened. It was a scene that had happened before. He would arrive on a visit bursting with things to tell her, and as if to ward him off center stage and reduce him to his proper place in the audience, she'd immediately read him one of Daniel's postcards followed by her testimony (as she was also doing now) about how thoughtful Daniel was. The injustice of the word "thoughtful" applied to his brother always stung him. By his calculations Daniel visited her one fifth as frequently as he did, and never alone, though he'd been divorced for years. Yet he was described as "thoughtful" simply because he wrote her little postcards about his inane career as an arts administrator.

When she was finally through with her tributes to Daniel, she began cataloging the pain that filled "the few days I have left before I'll be dead forever." Her large brown eyes looked fierce as she spoke, commanding his attention. He noticed that her dyed black hair was combed back, her makeup meticulously painted on her face. Clearly she had spent an enormous amount of time on her face—yet she didn't have a moment to ask about his promotion in the University Relations office, and when she finally asked him about his wife, she paused a few seconds (as she often did) as if it were so difficult to remember that her name was Cherise.

Slowly he felt himself withdraw until he was no longer listening to the individual words she spoke but had begun converting them into a general tone he responded to only when it went up a few degrees while she asked him a question or, much less frequently, when it stopped and he was expected to respond. It was a technique he'd developed over the years which he felt somewhat guilty about but knew was crucial for avoiding arguments. And that mustn't happen this time, or ever again. His memories were filled with horrible, screaming fights with her, not unlike the quarrels he used to have during his bad time with Cherise.

Around one o'clock she sat down in her La-Z-Boy to watch *The Young and the Restless*, the first of the soap operas that eventually led to her nap, and he excused himself.

"Where are you going?"

"I thought I'd take a swim."

"You're going to the pool?"

"Actually, I was planning to go to the beach."

"That dirty town beach?"

"Is that all right? Is that a problem for you?"

"It's fine. It's no problem at all," she said, indicating by the resigned nodding of her head that by selecting the beach over the swimming pool, which her friends and neighbors from the condominium complex used, he was again wounding her.

He changed into his suit quickly, not even bothering to comb his slightly receding brown hair as he normally did before going outside. He took a pink towel from the hall closet and the first shirt he found in his suitcase. He did remember to take his glasses and a copy of the alumni bulletin that had the article on his promotion he'd wanted to show his mother. At least Cherise had said she was proud of his promotion, although it meant only a slight increase in salary. "I should concentrate on her reaction and not worry about my mother's," he thought, as he left the condominium, where his mother was already transfixed by the TV.

Outside, in the bright sun, the other buildings in the complex extended in white planes as far as he could see, although he realized, with an ironic laugh at himself, that he couldn't see as far as he once could. For forty-one years he hadn't needed glasses, but six months ago, just after his birthday, his sight started declining. At the same time his hair began to gray and recede (he was still unsure whether to color it). It was as if in less than a year he'd gone from youth to middle age.

Across the street from the complex was the town beach—a white stretch of sand about a hundred yards long—bounded on one side by a fence and on the other by the white-and-blue casino. Most of the people at the beach were middle- or lower-middle-class residents of the town, many of them Italian or Eastern European immigrants. Already he could hear the concluding strains of "Volare" being played by a small dance band. Twenty or so elderly couples were dancing to it in a large open-air tent. Though some of the dancers looked feeble, on the whole they seemed to be having a good time. They made Steven feel better. Going to the beach was a good idea, he thought, and under the circumstances it was probably the best medicine he could have taken. When the band shifted to a snappy polka the old people began clapping their hands and dancing more spiritedly. Steven smiled. It was fun to watch but it would be too noisy to read the bulletin by the tent, so he moved. He walked past the boccie courts and swings, then past a number of occupied picnic tables shaded by pine trees, until he settled at a free table near the casino end of the beach.

Before reading the rest of the issue, he couldn't resist looking again at the article about his promotion, which consisted of four small paragraphs and a headshot of him smiling. Cherise had said it was a great picture, and he had to admit it was pretty flattering. He read the piece twice and was pleased. His mother would have liked it, too, especially since it had references to both his father's career as a successful banker and to her own years as a private-school English teacher. It was a well-written article, done by Mark Stem, a twenty-five-year-old who'd been in the department less than a year. He's already a better writer than I am, Steven thought a little nervously.

He flipped through the magazine looking for something else to read, while an old man with sky-blue eyes and a vaguely dreamy smile sat next to him. Steven smiled back briefly, and to be polite, waited a couple of minutes before moving two tables away. He was now next to the casino at the extreme end of the beach. He read the first paragraph of an article on last year's alumni donations drive (looking over guiltily a couple of times at the old man, who still hadn't moved his head an inch) when he heard a siren from a police car that was suddenly driving right over the sand. The car was going very fast and was followed ten seconds later by two other police cars. They drove on the firmer sand about fifteen feet from the water, scattering sea gulls and sandpipers, and parked at the opposite end of the beach. Steven closed the magazine and stood up. Was there a robbery, or a fight of some kind? He wondered why he hadn't heard any cries for help and so, of course, hadn't seen anything either. Already a small circle of people had formed in front of the police cars near the water. Walking toward them, Steven noticed that the dancing had stopped and that no one was playing boccie either. Most of the people at the beach were drifting toward the circle. Thirty feet away he asked an elderly woman in a faded purple bathing suit what had happened. She threw up her arms like a giant bird spreading its wings. He turned from her to one of the boccie players and asked the same question. The man shook his balding head, and Steven kept walking until he saw a boy with orange hair standing in a daze.

"You know what happened?"

"He went belly-up. I pulled him in," the boy said with an accent, pointing to the body of a man lying on the sand. Steven looked at the boy doubtfully. Was he lying? He seemed to be about fifteen and on the slender side but perhaps was strong enough to do what he'd said. Besides, who would be grotesque enough to lie about such a thing?

"Did he drown?"

The boy's lips twitched but he said nothing. Steven moved nearer the old man on the sand, in the center of the circle, whose eyes were half closed and whose stomach was puffed out like a blowfish. A policeman kept pounding his heart with his hand, while another put a new tube in his mouth.

"Anybody here have a towel?" a third policeman said, turning toward the crowd.

"I do," Steven said, handing it to the policeman, who immediately rubbed the chest and legs of the old man.

The police worked quickly and precisely. Steven was too nervous to watch them for long, however—only fifteen or twenty seconds at a stretch before he'd look at the crowd, at the two open-mouthed eight-year-old boys or at the little girl in the China-blue bathing suit staring as silently as the boccie players and the dancers. Then he made eye contact with a fiftyish woman with enormous blue eyes and thickly knotted gray hair and walked next to her.

"Is he going to make it?"

"I don't know. They say he has a faint pulse."

"Did he drown? Is that what happened?"

"I think he had a heart attack; that boy found him."

"It's crazy. I didn't hear anything. Why didn't anybody scream for help?"

"The boy was with him," she said, pointing again to the orange-haired boy standing next to an obviously distraught woman of indeterminate age who was talking to yet another policeman.

"He and that woman were with the man. Just thirty minutes ago they were taking his picture on the beach. They're Serbians and they're afraid to identify the man or themselves for some reason. Maybe they don't have the right papers to be here, I don't know. I said to her 'I'm Serbian too, what are you afraid of?' See her clutching the man's wallet? She doesn't want to give it up. Good God, I've seen three old ones pulled up from the water just since I've moved here. I pulled one up myself and I wasn't afraid. He's still alive today . . . an Italian. Not that anyone's ever given me any credit for it."

There was another siren, another whirling orange light. A big white-and-orange ambulance parked beside the police cars and five paramedics emerged from the truck carrying a stretcher and additional equipment. They asked for more room, and the circle silently expanded. They added new tubes, repositioned old ones, and continued pumping his heart. Steven kept watching the man for a sign of life. His eyes were half open and he sometimes seemed to be trying to assist them but Steven couldn't be sure. It occurred to him that he'd never seen a person die before. His father's stroke had happened six years ago, and he'd died before Steven could fly down to see him. How odd to have lived such a protected life while these children on the beach were seeing something he'd been spared until today.

Four of the paramedics began lifting the man onto the stretcher. The fifth was still working on his heart as they placed him in the ambulance. Steven turned to a policeman and asked him if he thought the man would live.

"Are you a reporter?"

"No, not at all. I'm just concerned."

"Can't say right now, could go either way. We'll know in about thirty minutes."

Steven nodded and walked away. He saw that the woman with the orange-haired boy was openly sobbing now as they got into a police car. The older woman with the huge blue eyes turned toward him.

"Are they going to be all right?" he asked.

"I don't know why she's so suspicious. You've got to trust somebody at some point. You've got to trust God or at least the police, don't you?"

She said this so unsympathetically it made him angry and he walked past her. Then he turned his attention to the ambulance, which still hadn't moved although it seemed a lot of time had gone by.

"Why isn't it moving?" he finally asked an old man he'd seen before playing boccie.

"They may be setting him up carefully in the truck. Or maybe he's gone already, and there's no reason to rush," he added with a little smile on his lips.

Ten minutes later the ambulance began to drive away slowly and Steven concluded that the man must have died. The people from the circle had already dispersed. Some were back in the water swimming, others were already dancing again to a waltz he couldn't identify. This must happen all the time, he thought, looking at the dancers. Maybe it was part of some fatalistic attitude they held in common, which explained how they could resume their activities right after the drowning.

At any rate, he wouldn't brood about it or try to judge them. Instead he decided to go back to the condominium. He took a few steps in that direction before something caught his eye. It was the pink towel he'd given the policeman, lying tangled in the sand. Should he bring it home? His mother might notice it was missing and complain, but when he walked a step or two toward it he couldn't bear to pick it up—although he'd felt secretly proud to have contributed it to the rescue effort. He wondered now if he should even mention what had happened to his mother. She often got upset hearing about other people's pain or disasters. Also, if he didn't say anything about it she might never realize the towel was missing since there were dozens of others in her hall closet. It seemed that saying nothing really would be the best policy, especially since he felt that he couldn't bear to touch the towel anyway and was already moving away from it.

When he opened the door to the condominium his mother was at her desk by the picture window looking at some papers. "The beach boy returns, at last. How was your swim?"

"O.K."

"I've just got Silverman's bill. What a swindler! Do you want to see it? Do you want to see what he charged me?"

"You need to get a new accountant."

"Wait till I show you what Dr. Walters charged me for my cataract treatment. He's in the medical mafia, too. Come here and look at this bill."

Steven walked toward her and looked at the bill, but in his mind's eye he was seeing the old man on the sand with the tubes in his mouth.

"Did you see that? Why does he do this to me? He acts so nice on the phone to hook me in and talks so sweetly while he examines me and then he sends me this. He's just like a male whore, if you ask me. I'm going to get rid of both of them. Starting tomorrow I'm getting a new knee man and a new cataract man, both."

"It's not that much. It's just a standard bill."

"Not that much? You must have much more money than I realize if you don't think he's trying to rob me with a bill like that. Of course, you can earn money, can't you? I can't. I'm on a fixed income that's getting eaten up all the time by this marvelous economy while I can barely get around to help myself. You don't realize, Stevie, but it's a fulltime job just keeping myself alive."

"You should get someone to help you. I've told you that. You have plenty of money and you've got to start spending some of it to help yourself. Believe me, you can definitely afford it."

"Not what they charge. They pretend to love you, too, and then they steal your jewelry or whatever else they can get their hands on."

She went on about the impossibility of getting honest, competent help, live-in or otherwise. Steven began hearing the tone again but it wasn't providing any relief from his mother or from the image of the old man on the sand, which was still fresh in his mind.

"Why are you pacing around, Stevie? I wish my legs felt good enough to let me pace, too, but they don't, and they probably never will."

"You don't understand. Something terrible happened on the beach."

He looked at her and saw her face turn toward him, her dark eyes opening up wide in concentration.

"What's this?"

"A man drowned."

"I'm sorry, darling, but it happens all the time."

"You don't understand. I was reading at the far end of the beach so I didn't see it happen or hear anybody cry for help, or I would have tried to save him myself. But then the police came, someone must have called them on a pay phone, and I ran down to see what happened. He'd had a heart attack and the police and the paramedics must have worked on him for a half-hour."

"Your father and I once watched something much worse than that at Passagille beach."

"I'm not trying to compete with you. It was just a shocking thing to see. I even got involved in a way. One of the cops working on him asked if anyone had a towel so I gave him mine."

"You mean you gave him my towel."

"Whatever."

"It wasn't a pink one with red embroidered poodles was it?"

"I don't know. What difference does it make?"

"Couldn't you have given him a less expensive one?"

"Do you hear what you're saying? Do you realize how absurd you sound? The man was dying and I was asked to help. I didn't think about how much the towel cost. You have twenty-two thousand others anyway, don't you?"

"Don't be fresh, Stevie. There's no reason to be fresh to me."

"O.K. But there's also no reason for you to be so stingy when you're really a very wealthy woman and there's no reason to be so inconsistent and . . . crazy with me about money. I mean you keep hiring new doctors like they're some kind of escort service, and that costs money, yet you complain when I give a cop a towel to try to save a man's life."

She turned her head away with a shocked expression on her face and Steven felt himself begin to shake.

"Look, I need to be alone for a little while to calm down. I'll be back in ten minutes," he said as he walked to the bathroom, swallowed two Tylenols, and then shut the door to his room.

After lying in bed for a few minutes he stopped shaking. He closed his eyes and the image of the old man returned briefly as a blur, then was gone again, and stayed gone. He was feeling much better now and reassured himself that he hadn't really lost his temper yet. Certainly he mustn't expect rational humanism from his mother at this point, nor should he let its absence make him mad at her. He reminded himself of his commitment to make this visit the one in which they didn't fight. Still, he thought he should wait awhile longer to be as calm as possible before leaving his room. He turned on the clock radio and to his amazement found a classical music station. Someone was playing a Debussy prelude softly, then later something that sounded like Satie. Steven closed his eyes again to listen and this time fell asleep.

When he woke up two hours later it was dark out. Immediately he left his room and found his mother in the kitchen by the sink holding her cane in one hand and boiling water with the other.

"The craziest thing happened. I turned on the radio to relax for a while and I fell asleep. I'm sorry I was away for so long. Anyway, I feel a lot better now."

She didn't speak.

"I told you I just needed some time by myself and now I'm back. I didn't plan to fall asleep and I'm sorry about that. So where were we? Which doctor were you telling me about?"

She said nothing. When he walked next to her he saw that she was crying—her face looking older and more frightened than he'd ever seen it.

"Mummy, what's the matter?"

"I'm sorry about what happened on the beach and that it upset you so much."

"I told you, I'm much better now."

"You're only here three days and now one of them's already gone and with that man on your mind all the time I thought I wouldn't get a chance to talk to you. Then you stayed in your room with the radio on and I was afraid to disturb you. I thought you'd get mad again or else were still mad at me and I've waited so long to see you."

"That was a misunderstanding about the radio," he said softly. He felt touched and scared and looked more closely at her, as if to be certain it was his mother speaking. Sometimes, especially after a drink or two, when he'd stare at people long enough they'd almost start to turn into other people. He thought this might happen now, that she might turn into the old man on the sand.

"Every day there's so much tragedy in the world . . . drowning, dying. The television's full of it but what can you do?"

"I don't know, Mummy." She looked more like herself now. The image of the old man was still gone.

"I feel like I'm drowning, myself, and no matter what I do, no matter how hard I fight, I'm going to die soon and it scares me so much." She stooped forward a little as if she were in a rocking chair and he embraced her and kissed her hair while she continued crying softly in his arms. But when they moved apart he felt himself burn with shame.

"I'm sorry for the things I said to you, all the things I ever said. I never should have said them," he quickly added. "Never."

"It doesn't matter," she said, half-smiling through her tears now and looking strangely pretty again. "It never did."

He looked at her, then past her out the window at the black sky flecked with distant lights. Then he hugged her tightly once more, tightly enough to feel her breathing, and for a moment he believed her.

MISTAKES

One of Single Booklovers' ideas for their spring banquet was to ask each guest to bring a book of their choice and leave it on the central table of the hotel dining room. Once the books were arranged, each guest could look through and select any book that the other guests brought as a gift for him or herself. We would all have the fun of giving and receiving, Ruth and Ray, who ran the organization, observed in their breathless invitation, and we would also learn something important about one another. Many of the guests brought motivational or inspirational books, some brought nature or New Age books, and there were also more than a few romance novels. I brought an extra copy I had of Jean-Paul Sartre's *Nausea*. Except for *The Selected Poems of Wallace Stevens*, it looked like the only real piece of literature on the table. That wasn't a good sign but I thought that maybe some of the other guests didn't want to give away a book they valued to a stranger. It was a thought, anyway, or a hope.

Ruth and Ray had other less intellectually ambitious ideas for their dinner. They offered a mystery gift to any couple who had the same birthday. The purpose, of course, was to give everyone a safe opening line to use during the cocktail hour. Soon a parade of fiftyish and older women (many of them considerably overweight) began asking me when my birthday was, while I, in turn, kept looking at a youthful blonde who was understandably quite oblivious to me, surrounded as she was by a tight circle of attractive men in their early thirties—at least ten years younger than me. It was all becoming slightly surreal, and immensely disappointing. I longed to get a drink from the bar in the lounge but the army of guests was rapidly multiplying and the line was at least twenty deep. Suddenly it occurred to me that Independence Hall and a bevy of other historical landmarks were less than two blocks from the hotel. I'd lived in Philadelphia (in Center City, no less) for more than a decade, but I'd never visited any of those august places. If I left now there would still be enough light out to see one or two of them, though it might still be drizzling out and I hadn't brought an umbrella. April really is turning out to be the cruelest month, I remember thinking.

Then I had another idea. When I first walked into the hotel I thought I'd seen a bar, a fairly quiet, unpopulated but definitely open bar. If the bar did exist, I could have a drink in peace and perhaps watch a ball-game, assuming they had a TV there, which would make returning to my apartment a lot easier.

I must have been more possessed by this idea than I realized for I immediately started to extricate myself from the dense crowd of birthday babbling booklovers—but before I'd moved ten feet I bumped into a fairly tall man and made him spill some of his drink. I apologized profusely and insisted that he let me buy him another. He smiled and was good-natured about it. He was about my age, maybe an inch or two taller, with very even white teeth.

"Making your getaway?" he said.

"Can't deny it. I'd have to say this isn't what I envisioned," I added.

"Oh, God no, it's a catastrophe. At least for me."

"Me, too. What a mistake."

"Well, it's inevitable," he said, or something like that. He told me his name was Evan, and I shook hands, being careful not to jeopardize the remainder of his drink that he was still holding. We talked for a few minutes and I discovered that he had brought the Wallace Stevens book. We laughed about that. Then I told him about the bar and invited him to have a drink with me there. I was going to make a joke about being glad I'd picked somebody up here but thought better of it.

The bar was more or less as I imagined it. There was even a basketball game on the TV on the wall. Perhaps because it was so gray outside, the bar was even more dimly lit than I'd thought. It was hard to tell for sure but as we drank our gins Evan's eyes looked green like mine or at least had green in them. He was still talking about mistakes, apparently seizing it as his theme of the evening. It had begun with the mistake of coming to this affair in the vain hope of meeting an attractive woman, which brought to mind the mistake of joining this absurd dating club in the first place. He made some self-deprecating joke about his life being a mistake, or a series of them, and I said something about his good sense of humor and what a useful weapon it was at times like these, but Evan insisted that, unfortunately, he wasn't the way I was describing him at all.

"The truth is I've never been able to tolerate mistakes in life or in art," he said, leaning in closer to me from across the table. "Not very well anyway. The problem is I've always been very good at spotting them. I think that's why I became an accountant. There's less ambiguity when you deal with figures."

"You mean in identifying mistakes?"

He smiled ironically.

"More about correcting them. When I find a mistake in someone's tax forms I'm usually saving them money or keeping them out of trouble. Figures don't lie—either they balance or they don't. But sometimes when you think you're correcting a mistake in your life, you're actually making things worse for yourself later on." He paused and looked at me. "Can I tell you a story?"

"Sure. Go ahead, but let me get another drink first," I said, running my fingers across my mustache and then gesturing toward the waiter, whose back was turned to us.

"You want one, too?"

"Sure," Evan said.

Though I only drink on occasion, I wanted another badly enough that I more or less tuned Evan out until the waiter brought them. After my first swallow, when my attention resurfaced, he was already deep into talking about his mother.

"She was a concert pianist who could never be consoled by a review, no matter how flattering, if she knew she'd played a wrong note or phrased a passage incorrectly. On the other hand, she was perfectly capable of suffering over the tiniest bit of unjustified criticism in a review no matter how heavily qualified. In her life apart from music she was just as perfectionistic."

"In what ways?" I said.

"In all ways. All things. Her cooking, her use of grammar, her appearance, of course. Her lips tortured her by being too thin, her front teeth by protruding a fraction too much."

"Was she a hypochondriac, too?"

"My God, yes. A scratch in her throat was a hideous assault on her being, a mild cavity was a death threat. Sleep, of course, was an impossibility. Her earplugs were of little use against the endless array of sounds she heard that relentlessly disturbed her. Even when she took her sleeping pills she never claimed to have slept more than an hour and a half in a single night."

I laughed, in spite of myself, then said I was sorry. Evan gestured dismissively, as if to say he was glad he had made me laugh.

"So where was your father in all this?" I said.

"In his own room. He slept there because he snored. So, of course . . ."

"No, I meant, was he a perfectionist like your mother?"

"He was very different. Mild-mannered, tolerant, much older than her. He was a fairly successful businessman and he loved to dote on my mother. He treated her like a child and, in a way, we all did. I don't know why I followed her nature instead of my father's, who was so emotionally undemanding. I think I made an association between her complaints and fears, and high drama. She was always the star at every family meal, the one who did almost all the talking. I can still see it so clearly: the three listeners—my father, my sister, and me—our eyes riveted on my mother as she mimicked one of her students or a conductor she was making fun of or a critic she detested. At some point we'd invariably begin laughing, not merely to please her, but because she was an excellent mimic and could be devastatingly funny.

"Wait a minute. I think I may be making her sound like a monster and that wouldn't be fair, that wouldn't be true at all. There was lots of affection and warmth in her—besides the charm and talent—and she did love us all in her childlike kind of way. And especially when I was younger that was enough for me. My father was much more mature than her, but she spent more time with me even if I often felt I was merely her audience. That's probably why she influenced me more about perfectionism, for example, and suffering over mistakes. But can I tell you my story now?"

"Sure," I said, thinking that he already had.

"It's not too much for you? Not too self-indulgent of me?"

"Not at all. It's interesting, and believe me, I'm already relating to it in my own way."

"It's not a long story, though it's in two parts. The first has to do with my love for the piano, of all things. Pretty far from accounting, huh?" he said, with a little laugh. "But I think I had a real talent for it once and even won a city-wide competition when I was seven. I remember that I was entranced with the sounds a piano could make and loved making up my own pieces on it the way other kids were fascinated with toys and games, or maybe it was something more than that. I simply felt whole when I was playing—natural and complete. Unfortunately, I made the mistake of studying with my mother. My memories of those lessons mostly involve her making me repeat passages over and over until they were error-free. It was horrifying to be confronted with my own mistakes. I'd begin to yell or cry until the lessons would finally end. Eventually my father interceded for me and I stopped studying with her, and never studied again, actually, with anybody else. Once I was freed from practicing with my mother, I began to go to the playground and became a little sports fanatic. I got a lot of pleasure from sports over the years, especially basketball, though my fear of missing shots often kept me from shooting as much as I wanted or even as much as the team needed. The point is, I lived out a pretty normal childhood and adolescence, playing sports, pursuing girls, and avoiding music courses—which is why I became a math major. But I still had my love for music and, when my mother wasn't around, would continue improvising and making up my pieces on the piano, though by the time I started doing that I couldn't read music anymore and couldn't write them down.

"O.K., I'm about half done now. Let me flash forward to my midtwenties. I'm a C.P.A. and still a closet pianist having an average amount of success with women when suddenly I fall in love—deeply, crazily in love for the only time in my life—with Danielle, and that's the second part of my story."

He had finished his new drink and I looked at him more closely while he spoke and decided that he definitely did have green in his eyes, more than I'd realized, in fact.

"I met her at the office about a year after I started working for my first firm. She was starting out as a paralegal and she came in to have her taxes done. And you thought there was nothing sexy about accounting. She had shoulder-length black hair, extraordinary blue eyes and clear skin. The funny thing is, when we started talking—beyond the mere professional stuff we had to do—we discovered we both loved classical music. After I filed her taxes (because at work I've always done everything by the book and there were company rules about dating clients) I invited her to a piano recital. I can still remember the program: Haydn, Brahms, Prokofiev, Scriabin. I didn't even attempt to touch her the first few times we went out. She dazzled me! She had incredible energy, good humor, intelligence, kindness, and tact, and a refreshing self-confidence—a magical balance of masculine and feminine traits. It served her well—she became a pretty successful divorce lawyer. You see, I kept up with her, I followed her life long after I was out of it . . ."

"You hear men use the word goddess to describe a certain kind of woman and it sounds like so much garbage, but then you meet one and it's a humbling, almost terrifying kind of experience. It was really hard for me to believe she might like me, that I could ever even touch her. But on our fourth night out there was suddenly no more ambiguity. Her eyes and smile were directed wholly at me, and her words kept reassuring me that it wasn't an illusion—that she could be mine.

"We ate at the Orson Welles restaurant near Harvard Square. Do you know it?"

"No. I think I heard about it, though."

"It was a very chic place in its day. I don't know if it exists anymore. We walked slowly through Cambridge, then she suggested we go to a dance club (something I'd never done before), so the mere act of dancing with Danielle became infinitely exotic.

"We were on the floor dancing to one of the Beatles' ballads—'Girl' or

'In My Life,' I think—when we began to kiss. In my memory neither one of us was the aggressor—it was a simultaneous kiss. But shortly afterwards she said, very simply, and neither cruelly nor apologetically, 'Not like that,' and proceeded to show me by example how my tongue should interact with hers. 'There, that's good,' she said, smiling at me happily. But my mind reeled in anger from being corrected in such a delicate matter, from somehow being accused of making such an elemental mistake. I was able to repress my rage for a while, but when we returned to my apartment it started to come out in a number of pointedly sarcastic, utterly mean comments I made about her. It's odd—I knew what I was doing was horrible, but I couldn't stop it. I apologized profoundly the next day and she continued to be friends with me for a while, but she'd seen something in me that scared her and our romance was through. Shortly after I realized it was over, I composed a piano piece for her but of course I didn't know how to write it down," he said with a quick laugh, "and she never heard it, anyway."

We were quiet for a while. I wanted another drink but I didn't think it was the right time to get the attention of the waiter, who again had his back turned to us. I thought I should say something consoling to Evan but I couldn't think what would be right. "That's a sad story" or "I'm sorry that happened to you," I almost said. Then I started thinking about things in my own past, mistakes I'd made and so forth, but I didn't want to go down that road, either. What I needed was a transition but it never came to me. Finally, I said, "That's a hell of a story. I'm glad you told me," and then said that I sympathized and identified with him, and he thanked me for listening to him. More silence. Finally I pointed to the basketball game on TV and asked him if he followed the pros and who he liked in the playoffs. It was awkward, it was inadequate, and I felt that in some way I was probably disappointing him but I couldn't come up with anything else.

Fortunately Evan watched the rest of the quarter with me, making a comment or two about the Sixers every minute or so. He seemed to believe in their future more than I did. I remember there was 4:51 left in the third quarter when we started watching—but of course that was in basketball time. With all the time-outs, fouls, and commercials it was more like twenty-five minutes.

After the quarter ended we stretched and I yawned. Then I told Evan

I'd enjoyed it but that I was heading back to my apartment. He asked me where I lived and I told him a few blocks from the museum, just off the parkway. Evan's apartment was in Center City, near the Academy of Music. I asked him if he were going to try his luck again at the SBL dinner, and he laughed and said he didn't think so, that he just planned to stay in the bar and watch the fourth quarter. I wished him luck, I wished the Sixers luck, I stood up and extended my hand, and he stood up and shook it, and then he suggested we exchange phone numbers in case we ever wanted to have another drink. I was somewhat surprised but I found a pen and scrap of paper (which I thought would be used under very different circumstances), tore it in half, and exchanged the information. Then I shook his hand again, we both smiled and said goodbye, and I walked out of the bar down the bright hall and out of the hotel.

When I got home my apartment was unusually cold and quiet, as if a blanket of snow had fallen while I was away. "April in Antarctica," I said under my breath as I paced around. I looked out the windows, but nothing much was going on in the street. Most of what I saw outside were the sides of other buildings. I walked into my studio and checked my answering machine. I'd responded to a number of personals in *Philadelphia Magazine* but no one had called back yet. Then I turned on the TV just to fill up my apartment with some noise. I heated up some leftover Chinese food and ate it while I watched TV, and felt O.K. for a while until the nostalgic soundtrack for a watch commercial made me think about my ex-wife, which in turn reminded me of Donna. Then I got up from my La-Z-Boy and fixed myself a gin which I drank slowly until, an hour later, I was able to fall asleep.

That night I had an odd dream. I was walking through a park with Evan. It was a city park, unusually large with a lake in it where men were rowing boats. I was talking animatedly to Evan but every time I tried to look at him he turned his face away. The last time I looked, a black scarf was completely covering his face.

• • • • • • • • • •

The next three days were pretty routine. No more strange dreams, no more Antarctic apartment, nothing particularly humiliating at work. But

I didn't like how much I was thinking about Donna, and the quiet in my apartment, which I often found comforting, was making me feel vaguely panicky. I called a couple of former girlfriends just to have someone to talk to for a few minutes, but nobody was home. Then, I opened my address book and a minute later surprised myself by calling Evan. I couldn't remember the last time I'd called a man just to talk and it was pretty awkward at first. Evan must have sensed what I was feeling because he quickly said he was glad I'd called and that he wasn't doing anything either. It may have been Evan who suggested we meet for a drink.

We agreed that we should meet somewhere midway between where we lived, but that still left a lot of places to choose from. Perhaps because it doesn't have much of a night life, Philadelphia is one of those cities where eating and even drinking are taken very seriously and treated like an art form. The city is overloaded with places to eat and drink, and restaurants and bars are reviewed as if they were books or movies in newspapers and in the city's magazines. As a result, people become more finicky than they need to be, and we were no exception. We kept discussing places and then dismissing them for one reason or another until I finally said why don't we just meet at the hotel bar where we'd gone before and Evan laughed and said fine, it sounded good to him.

A half hour later we were at a table there, with the same dim lights and the brighter light from the hall glowing like a distant fire, with the same zombie waiter, but with no game and so no TV on this time. We sipped our drinks and found it a little difficult to talk at first. Then I said, "I have to say I'm surprised to be here with you."

"What do you mean?" he said.

"I'm surprised that I called you. Not that you're not interesting and perfectly charming but that my whole life I've met interesting men from time to time in bars, or in business situations, but I've never followed up and seen any of them a second time, socially. Maybe that was a mistake to let people pass out of my life that I shouldn't have just because they were men, people who might have become friends. You know, you told me about your mistakes last time. Maybe that was one of mine."

"Actually, I was wondering what you thought of my little story. I remember you said that you identified," he said raising his eyebrows hopefully.

"I did, in a way, but I also think it's different with me. I mean to judge from your story it sounds like you were more hurt by making mistakes than by finding them in others. I think I had the opposite problem."

"You were a faultfinder, a balloon breaker?"

I laughed. "I guess that's true, and one time in particular I definitely was."

"Why don't you tell me about it?"

I laughed again. "Could you really bear to listen to it?"

"Why not? My God, after telling you my story, I insist on it."

I shrugged. I guess I must have wanted to tell him for some reason or I wouldn't have brought it up. "Like you, it's about a woman I met when I was a lot younger."

"What was her name?"

"Her name was Donna, and I met her shortly after I got divorced."

"You married young?"

"Young and badly. I met my wife at art school when I was twenty-one, married her at twenty-two, divorced at twenty-three."

"You're an artist then?"

"No, I'm a designer. I didn't mean to deceive you. There's very little art in my work."

He ignored my small joke, or maybe he said, "There's no art in mine." Then he asked if I worked for a company.

"I freelance now, work for ad agencies, do some magazine work."

"Sorry to interrupt you. I'm kind of a fact freak. If I'd designed the profiles for Single Booklovers there would have been ten times as many questions on them. But sorry, I really do want to hear your story."

"It's not much of one."

"But one I'd really like to hear. You were talking about meeting Donna shortly after your divorce."

"The thing about my ex-wife was that, while she definitely had her share of pathology, and it was a bitter blow when she divorced me, I couldn't help idealizing her in a lot of ways. She was still my notion of how a woman should behave. The way she dressed and handled herself in social situations, the way she carried herself—her carriage, if people still use that word. She was my standard for the social graces—or 'femininity,' I suppose—and that meant more to me than I realized.

"I met Donna in a bar when I used to try to meet women that way. She was working as a hospital technician in Philadelphia for not very much money. Her parents weren't well off and had three other children, so Donna always had to go without good clothes and vacations and good schools and always had to worry about paying her bills. In many ways she was the most contradictory person I ever met. She was Catholic and very religious but she loved sex, and as far as her body went, she was extremely uninhibited."

"What did she look like?"

"Reddish-blond hair, big green eyes. I was very attracted to her, more attracted to her than I was to my wife. And since I'd always been something of a prude, her uninhibitedness did more than embarrass me. It was also exciting and freed me up in a lot of ways."

"Sounds like she might have been the perfect transitional object, as they say."

"If only I'd been a transitional-object kind of man," I said, laughing. "But I wanted love again right away, perfect love. I was young and wounded and didn't know how to tolerate life without it, and also how did I know when it could happen again?"

"You were right there."

"So because of all that, that's when I started to let her little imperfections get to me."

"Like what?"

"It was lots of things, little things that my wife never would have done, like the way she sometimes used double negatives, or said 'good' when she should have said 'well' or eliminated the *g*'s at the end of words or, God forbid, sometimes spoke while she was chewing food."

"That pretty much covers speech."

"But I also loved her voice. It was warm and soft and musical and unafraid to say things I was starved to hear. It was a paradox. In the same way, I loved her body. I was immensely excited by it but I was irritated by her pigeon-toed walk, by the way she swung her arms back and forth too rapidly while she walked, by the way she blew her nose so loudly and without apology or any trace of self-consciousness, even by the way she'd yawn so often."

"Yawns can be pissers, can't they? Hostile, passive-aggressive little acts. Yawns have troubled me, too," he said.

"I don't think it was that way with Donna. I think she was just untrained in those so-called social graces, which I now think are more like social disgraces. At first I thought she talked the way she did to try to be cool or make some kind of social statement, and sometimes I thought she did it just to annoy me, but when I met her family, who talked pretty much the same way, I realized it was just how she was brought up. I remember thinking what an impeccable lady my wife had really been, and why hadn't I appreciated her more? Other times I would wonder what my wife would think of Donna if she had dinner with her and what would she think of me.

"Intellectually, there were more serious problems. Her politics were too conservative; she knew nothing about literature, classical music, or modern art, although she was very perceptive about people and she was curious and smart, with lots of energy and enthusiasm for things. When I took the time to play records for her or point out things at a museum she seemed to grasp them surprisingly well.

"I tried breaking up with her a number of times—we had some terrible fights—and a couple of times I did leave for a few days but I always came back. A year went by and then she got pregnant."

"Oh dear."

"Exactly." I looked away for a moment at the far right corner of the bar. Someone was noodling on the piano. It sounded like "Twilight Time," the old Platters' tune. The man was just good or bad enough that I couldn't really tell if it were his job to play or if it were just a customer feeling his oats. I raised my eyebrows sarcastically and Evan smiled his ironic smile. Then I finished my drink and went on.

"At that time abortions were much less controversial than they are today. Since our relationship was unstable, and neither of us had much money, it seemed the only route to go. But Donna wouldn't hear of it. To her it was a sin, a killing pure and simple. I tried all the arguments. I said it wasn't a human, that 'it' didn't think yet and nothing that didn't think was human. I told her she was just brainwashed by her religion, that having a baby now would ruin both our lives, but none of this cut any ice with Donna.

"'Don't you want to have a child?' she said."

"'Sure, eventually, just not now.'"

"'I thought you were such a creative person.'"

"'What's creative about morning sickness, contractions, and hospital bills?'"

"'What's so important about painting pictures compared to bringing a human being into the world and caring for it right?'"

"Then I'd get angry and eventually start yelling, but she wouldn't budge. I thought her position was based on ignorance, that she was just a victim of her class and church, and she said I was cold and heartless and afraid. Finally, three months into the pregnancy she said she was through with me, that it wasn't my problem anymore, that I should just put it out of my mind. I remember screaming at her before she left my apartment for the last time, 'You're making a horrible mistake.'

"Somehow I pretty much blocked out her pregnancy for the next few months but I wasn't able to stop thinking about her so easily. Instead of gradually thinking about Donna less, I thought about and missed her more. Suddenly the things that irritated me about her, her grammatical mistakes or awkward way of walking, seemed either inconsequential or else authenticating proof of an honest, original soul.

"I thought it was wrong to call her; I thought it was weak of me but I couldn't help myself. She agreed to meet me at a coffee shop. She was seven months pregnant and looked every bit of it. She was nervous, too, and bitter, but still able to crack a joke or two. And when she laughed, she looked so good I felt a sharp stab of pain or longing.

"Nothing had changed in her thinking. I could see that right away. There was no point in even asking if she'd consider giving up the baby for adoption. And when I started talking about getting together again and moved my fingers through her hair she pulled away from me. There could be nothing like that, no talk of anything like that unless we got married and I helped her raise our child. I nodded and said nothing for a while. I was reasoning with myself in the way I reasoned with myself then. I was too young to get married, much less to be a father. I would lose my freedom; I would sabotage my career, though I'd already dropped out of art school and was working for an ad agency, as bored by it then as I am now. Yet somehow I convinced myself it would destroy my life.

"My line of reasoning lasted less than a minute and a half. At the end of it I was ready to back away from her again, though I did say I wanted to pay the hospital bills and help support the baby.

"'I won't take more than half if you're willing to give it. Thanks,' she added with a brief look of relief in her eyes and I realized then, as I hadn't before, how frightening this all was for her.

"So that's the way I made the decisions not to marry, or to raise my child—in a moment's reasoning in a coffee shop. And that's about what I know of mistakes."

"So did she have the baby; did it turn out all right?" Evan asked. I looked around myself and noticed that the colors in the room had deepened to something like a dark blue, that as far as the room went it really was twilight time.

"She had the baby. It was a healthy boy she named Mark. She let me see him a few times shortly after he was born. I could see she was a terrific mother. That didn't surprise me. And I followed through on the money. I told my parents about it, and good liberals of the day that they were, they agreed to help me. But before Mark had his first birthday, something completely unforeseen happened—at least unforeseen by me. Donna met a man, an older man in the furniture business, and within a few months they got married. He was proud and possessive and didn't want me near his house. He also told me he wouldn't accept any of my money. Eventually Donna had two more children with him. A boy and a girl. As far as I know they're still married. I say as far as I know because I haven't heard from her in years. But for a long time, longer than I ever would have imagined, I thought with regret that her husband could have been me, you know, it could have been me."

Evan moved his free hand slightly forward towards me. "And did you ever marry again?"

"No. Two or three times things got serious and once I lived with a woman for a while, but no. And I never had any other children, or even made another woman pregnant. I was very careful not to make that mistake again," I said, smiling ironically myself.

"I think you were very honorable about the whole business, and quite courageous, especially considering how young you were, to follow through on the money like that. Not many would have done that."

"I'm glad her life turned out well, from what I know of it, believe me."

"I also think you're much too hard on yourself."

"And I thought the same thing when I heard your story. I meant to tell you that. You were very young when you ruined things with Danielle and much younger when you gave up studying the piano."

"But your story is much more serious than mine. My God—the birth of a child, the fate of so many people. It totally eclipses mine."

"I wouldn't say that. You gave up music and the woman of your dreams. What could exceed that?"

Evan didn't say anything. At first he looked to be considering what I had said, but after a while I thought he was thinking about something else. Then he said, "I meant to ask you, if it's O.K., if you ever got to see your son again, when he grew up?"

"Once. I'd found out what school he went to and told a story to some people there so I could see a picture of him in the yearbook. A few days later I waited for him outside his classroom (he was about twelve then) and I followed him through the playground to his bus stop. He was a beautiful, beautiful kid. I'd have to say he was really quite flawless."

Evan shook his head slowly from side to side in a gesture meant to convey sympathy. There seemed to be another question in his eyes, which I thought I knew, so I said, again, that I was glad I'd seen my son and glad that he looked so good, which was what was most important, and not my own regret that I never got to know him, or see him again.

After that, I don't remember much about our conversation. We made some small talk, we made the obligatory remarks about staying in touch and getting together again. I couldn't tell how much either of us meant it though I knew I certainly wasn't closing the door on it. We shook hands, perhaps more firmly than usual because as men we had to pack whatever emotion we felt into that brief gesture, and then I turned to face the stronger fire-like light in the hall.

When I was alone a wave of sadness went through me that seemed to ride me home. Once you talk about your life in a certain way, once you deliver up the mistakes of your life to another, a curious paralysis sets in. You have this knowledge but you also have an emptiness that covers it like a wall of ice because you know that no matter what you say it won't really alter anything, that ultimately only your mistakes remain.

In my apartment I saw the sides of buildings, the closed windows of buildings, the unblinking electric green and red lights of my answering machine, like frozen little jewels. I watched some TV, then went to sleep. I remember being vaguely afraid I'd dream about Donna, some variant of a recurrent dream where we've reconciled a few years after we broke up and were making love ecstatically but also angrily in my parent's house.

But I didn't dream about her. Instead, shortly before I woke up I dreamed about Evan. We were walking in a kind of park that was filled with thick sheets of ice stretching all around us for miles. We walked in silence for a long time until I saw an opening in the ice where a little tree had emerged. When we got closer to the tree we saw that it had sparkling blue flowers. "It's miraculous," I said, as I bent down to touch the tree.

"Well, it's April," Evan said.

I woke up feeling strangely pleased and energetic. I had slept later than usual, and when I looked out the window I could see people on the street already on their way to work. I began to hurry so I could be one of them.

THE PARK

Don't think I leave for the outer dark,
Like Adam and Eve put out of the park.

— ROBERT FROST

At first it was like an invitation from the sky which there was no possibility of refusing. He began going to the park every day knowing something important would happen. He found a favorite pond, later a favorite bench facing the pond, and waited surrounded by a group of delicate, oriental-looking trees with their red and green, gold and orange leaves. Then her image appeared before him one day like a delicate little tree itself. It was as if she were born in the park, as if that were her true home and her life at the travel agency a mere illusion. Vince wasn't even surprised or disappointed when the image left him a few moments later—he already knew what to do.

The next afternoon he returned to the agency where he'd met her just the week before. He'd gone there twice, once to buy a ticket to Chicago, then to buy one to New York. At the time he figured he needed to travel since it had gotten so quiet in his apartment building where he hadn't yet met anyone.

This time he didn't go inside but watched her through the street-level window, seeing mostly the crown of her yellowish hair. When she was ready to leave work, he followed from a safe distance till she got to the Metrolink stop, pressing himself against the side of a lamppost and waiting until she got on her train heading west.

He began going to the agency on the pretext of planning a winter vacation in Bermuda or Jamaica and soon started finding out some things about her. Her name was Janice and she was twenty-five, quite young, but not necessarily too young for him. She lived alone near the airport outside the city and seemingly had traveled everywhere, taking advantage of her reduced travel rates, she'd said, laughing. Her teeth protruded a little, yet this didn't inhibit her from having a full smile, which Vince found extremely appealing.

On his third or fourth visit Janice started asking Vince some questions, too. What exactly did he do? He told her that after his mother died he'd inherited some money and eventually had come to St. Louis a month ago to start a small business. "Why here?" she asked. There were so many better places to start a business back East, she would think. Because he'd had some happy years here before his parents moved, he said. Also, he knew it was a buyer's real estate market in St. Louis and he was interested in buying a house and settling down. His parents had bought a wonderful house here, but then they sold it to make money and moved East. He wanted to buy a house and *stay* in it, he said. She seemed impressed by that and by the time he left her office he wished he'd asked her to lunch.

He went directly home and watched the sunset over the park, seeing an image of Janice's toothy smile above the multi-colored trees, then later the interplay of moon and clouds like a mother holding a child. When he looked more closely, he saw Janice's profile in the moon and knew he would have to talk to her tomorrow and certainly, this time, invite her to lunch.

While he was shaving the next morning, he wondered what he would say when she'd inevitably ask him some more questions about his life. Since he wasn't working now and hadn't had a history of remarkable jobs, there wasn't much to talk about there. He'd been one of those students whose ambition was genuinely intellectual, and even spiritual, but definitely not material. He was like his parents that way: they had had only minimal experience with the working world. Their money, like his, had been inherited. They were fearful and suspicious of society in general and the business world in particular. That much Vince knew. But he couldn't tell if they created his own similar fears, or simply had the ability to understand them. They'd had him late in life, after a miscarriage and years of trying for a child, and seemed to guard him like a jewel. Yet he loved them deeply and often thought they were the only truly kindred spirits he'd ever met. Should he talk to Janice about them or focus more on his own life (since his parents were both dead now) and his plans for the future?

Perhaps there was one thing he definitely should tell Janice about his past—"the genius hour." The few people he had told seemed to find it quite intriguing. Every day, beginning with his freshman year in high school, his parents insisted he have at least one hour of contact a day with a great mind. It was one of the few things, besides basic honesty and not driving while drunk, they ever demanded of him. The hour could be served, as it were, in a variety of ways. He could listen to an hour of Beethoven or Bach, or go to a first-rate museum and look at Rembrandts or Picassos, or he could read an hour of Kant, Shakespeare, Spinoza, etc. The important thing was developing the discipline to do it every day until it became a habit. Though his parents checked on him, and two or three times a week listened to music or read and discussed philosophy with him, much of the genius hour was done on the honor system. But there were few times he didn't do it on his own, even during his college years while he was away from home. It was only after his father's heart attack that he stopped doing it regularly. Yes, he would definitely tell Janice about that, if she agreed to have lunch with him.

Inviting her wasn't as easy as Vince had hoped. He hesitated on the phone until he could sense Janice beginning to get exasperated, then blurted it out. She surprised him by suggesting they meet in an hour and a half during her lunch break. But this was said in such a casual way, as if he were her college roommate, that he felt deflated and wondered if she wanted him to know that in her mind this meeting had absolutely no romantic potential.

He remembered thinking there was no time to indulge such worries, no time for anything other than to shower, shampoo, and get dressed. He decided to wear a blue shirt, because his mother had always said it set off his blue eyes to great advantage, and having decided that much, he continued to pick blue as the color of his jeans and sports jacket.

He felt that he was racing too much, getting too nervous, so he stopped and gazed at the park for a moment from his bedroom window. It looked wise under the full sun. "That's where it all began," Vince said to himself. Then he left for the Greek-style diner that she'd suggested. She couldn't have picked a more pedestrian place but he tried not to interpret that as a bad sign. He had to stay strong and positive and reassure himself. At least I'm tall, he thought, as he approached the door of the restaurant, and that's almost always something. And wasn't it also true that he was intelligent and relatively well-read and, for now, financially independent, and that he had slept with a number of attractive women? The problem there had been his always wanting it to lead to something emotionally important and his pressing for that goal too quickly. His parents had told him that even geniuses don't matter much unless their gift helps or sustains people in a lasting way, and Vince felt the same about relationships. He made a mental note not to demand too much of Janice too fast, were he lucky enough to get involved with her.

She arrived a few minutes later, in a shortish black dress with gold hoop earrings and a matching necklace. She looked smart—she always looked smart and acted calm. She didn't seem to be the slightest bit nervous as she slid into the booth the way she slid into her swivel chair at work. He noticed, too, that she spoke to him in the same voice she used on the agency phone. Was she still thinking of him as a client, and of this as some kind of business lunch? He closed his eyes for a moment and concentrated on the image of her he had seen in the park when she appeared as an Eve-like figure of destiny in his life.

When he opened his eyes she had a puzzled look on her face and he wondered how long his eyes had been closed. "Is something the matter?" she asked.

Vince felt nonplused. He had to explain but how could he without lying? He said he'd been visualizing part of Forest Park because it made him feel good to do that.

"Are you a nature lover?" she said, still in her pleasant professional voice. Her Greek salad had arrived and she was already eating it in a perfectly relaxed way, whereas he felt befuddled by his Gyro plate and wished he had ordered something easier to eat. "Do you know the names of the different trees and flowers and what not?"

"Some of them, not many. That's not really why I go to the park."

She raised her eyebrows as if still puzzled, and he explained that he went to the park to get ideas.

"What kind of ideas?" she said.

"Ideas and . . . feelings about myself and life in general, and how I fit into it. That's what the park gives me."

She momentarily looked away, and he began thinking it might all be over with her, all be vanishing as her image did that day in the park.

Suddenly she turned toward him and looked him straight in the eyes. "I know what you mean about wanting to know how to fit into life. When I first started working in the agency, I couldn't stop flying."

For a moment he thought she knew how to fly like a bird or an angel, but she meant traveling in planes, of course. It began with her trying to take advantage of her reduced employee rates by flying a lot to the Caribbean but continued because she was lonely then and traveling was something to do that could give her life structure. "That's what I thought you were doing, too, when you kept buying plane tickets."

"I did that before I really discovered the park . . . but I used to do something else to give myself structure," he said, and then began telling her about the genius hour.

She followed him closely with her eyes while he spoke, which made him feel oddly important, then looked unusually animated when she answered him. "That's really neat the way they wanted you to develop your mind and all, and the way you stuck with it. Maybe you should keep doing it. I mean, why stop?"

Vince looked at her closely, himself, and felt transfixed.

"Would you consider the park? Would you consider going there with me sometime and just seeing what happens?"

"Thanks, that sounds nice, but I'm just so busy lately."

"I know it sounds a little odd. I know there's always a resistance to trying new things that we have to overcome, but believe me the rewards are immeasurable. There's a wonderful world in the park, a magical world where you can transcend the normal fog we walk around in, and pierce through to a different level of perception. There's a . . ."

"There's something else," she said cutting him off. "There's a special guy in my life and he might have trouble understanding why I'd go to the park with you, you know? See, I spend almost all my free time with him."

"I see."

He felt a pressure shoot up near his eyes, stopping perhaps a quarter inch from his eyeballs. It was all he could do not to scream. Somehow, five minutes later, after she'd finished her pecan pie, he walked her back to the agency. He could scarcely feel his feet, while a pins-and-needles sensation was resonating everywhere in his body, as if it had replaced his blood and flesh and he was all discordant nerve now.

She didn't comment on the way he walked or looked, but he turned his head away slightly so she wouldn't get a direct view of his eyes. He said good-bye and turned into an almost blinding sun streaming directly at him as he started to walk home.

So she had someone else. He'd never had a chance then. He stopped walking around his living room and sat down on the sofa, so lost in thought he barely noticed the park, though it was shimmering under the full sun. Then he got up from the sofa. What if she merely said she had a boyfriend just to get rid of him. Was that possible? Foolish to wonder about that now, though. Either way, she'd made it clear she wanted little to do with him. And was there such a great wonder there? He was tall (sometimes in the park he felt like a tree himself) which would be good for a tall woman, but she wasn't tall. Besides his height there was probably nothing outstanding about his appearance. His mother had loved his blue eyes and told him he was handsome, but that hardly meant other people thought so. The women he'd slept with had not said as much as he wanted (though he always yearned for a lot, he knew), and when they did he couldn't tell if they were merely flattering him. He could believe only in his parents' praise, but paradoxically, that was why you could also grow to distrust your parents. For what did their love do but paint a false or distorted picture of the world, since no one else would ever love you half, or a quarter, as much. And what was the purpose of this great early love in your life if they were going to die while you were still young, as his parents had before he was thirty? How was he to fill up all the years that were left him?

He was glad when the dark came. He was glad when he could lie in his bed and close his eyes at last and let sleep come. He fell asleep easily enough, but woke up with a jolt at 2:30 in the morning. It was as if he had been dreaming a long, puzzle-like dream and had woken up with the knowledge of the final piece. His lunch with Janice had not been in vain. The purpose of meeting her was not simply his own humiliation and defeat—far from it! Instead, it was that she might tell him, as she had during lunch, to resume the genius hour. That she should be so emphatic about its value and the importance of his returning to it instead of the park, which she scarcely mentioned, that she should say to him, "Why ever stop?" Why indeed? Stopping the genius hour was the worst thing he had ever done to himself, and now this message was sent through Janice, as if by some higher force, to set him back on the right path.

Tears came to his eyes as he thought about why he *had* stopped. In essence, he hadn't thought he could do the genius hour without his father being alive. It seemed to be something that was so connected to his parents that, when one of them died, the spell was broken and he lacked the will to continue. Then after his mother died, his will to do it left him completely. It was a step he was incapable of taking, but now a step he suddenly needed to take again.

How much time had he lost? It hadn't been part of his daily life for at least five years. Well, now that he wasn't working, now that he had the time and money for at least a year before he would have to work, he'd spend six genius hours a day, everyday, to make up for the lost years.

He began turning on all the lights in his apartment. He hardly knew where to start. Finally he decided to continue where he thought he'd left off, by finishing *The World as Will and Representation* by Schopenhauer, which he'd abandoned around page 100 five years ago, just after his father's heart attack. Certainly it wasn't easy reading (he had forgotten, for example, what the "Principle of Sufficient Reason" was), yet his concentration was so unusually intense that he was able to understand most of what he was reading and to read for two straight hours before he felt the need to stop.

After Schopenhauer, he listened to three of Bach's unaccompanied cello suites, then to Mahler's "Das Liede Von der Erde," whose haunting finale seemed to recreate in musical terms the experience of dying. He grieved for his parents, then, seemed to see them smiling at him in the sun rise's silver-white points of light. After that he fell asleep, but resumed reading Schopenhauer after lunch in his kitchen until he reached his six hours. He repeated the routine of reading, music, and reading for the next two weeks, always pushing himself until he finished his hours.

Meanwhile, the leaves were still mostly out and full of color, but he'd stopped going to the park. He seldom even looked at it through his windows. It was as if one night it had gotten up and moved away from him, so that when he did look now the park seemed to be quite far away. Only occasionally would he wonder why he didn't go there anymore, and when he did, the reasons came to him quickly. If the park had a purpose, it was to lead him to Janice, whose purpose, in turn, had been to lead him back to the genius hour. That purpose had been served. Moreover, it hurt him to remember the look on her face when he told her about the park and finally her rejection when he asked her to go there with him. Perhaps in addition to telling him to resume the genius hour, she was also trying to tell him to stop putting his faith in the park. To move on. What had the park really ever done for him? The park didn't love or educate him, the way his parents had, the way the genius hour was doing now.

It seemed easy not to think of the park, but at night he couldn't help dreaming about it. He might read all day, but at night he dreamed about the park. He would be on the bench by the pond, or walking deeper into the forest with the bright leaves blowing around him. Sometimes one of his parents would be with him. In one dream both of them were sitting on the bench laughing at a dog that was doing tricks in the pond. Whenever he had such dreams they would make him think much more about the park than he wanted to the next day. One afternoon while he was reading he found he couldn't stop looking at the park through the living room windows, until finally he got up from his chair and pulled down the venetian blinds. Then he pulled the blinds shut in each of his other two rooms. There had been way too much light in his apartment, anyway. Now with a few flicks of his wrist he could keep the park out almost completely.

But that night, he had his most powerful dream yet of the park. He was walking in the woods when he heard his mother's voice calling from a field up ahead. "We're here," she said, referring to herself and his father. "We're here." It was so strong a dream that when it was over it seemed to pull him out of bed, until the next thing he knew he had put his clothes on and was walking past the quizzical-looking doorman, across the street toward the park.

It was almost completely dark, except for the half moon, and there were hardly any cars on the highway. He knew he should walk slowly to avoid falling but he could hardly keep from hurrying, moving as much by memory as by sight, while trying to keep alive the sound of his mother's voice in his mind.

There was a field near the pond, above and to the left of it, which he had sometimes walked through. Of course there were several—perhaps many—fields in the park, but it would make sense for his parents to choose the one nearest his favorite spot in the park if there were going to be any sort of meeting or communion. Besides, it would be impossible for him to find, much less explore, the other fields tonight.

He was walking through a clearing toward the bridge that led to the pond, when he heard a rustling sound. The shock of it made him stumble and almost fall. He stood still and, looking toward his right, heard, then half-saw, someone walking his dog and talking to it. It was a man with a flashlight (which Vince wished he, himself, had taken), very possibly someone from his building. It surprised Vince that he was not alone, that other people, even at 4:00 in the morning, were also in the park. He stared in the direction of the man (who had been keeping a steady stream of chatter going at the dog) until his voice faded away. Then slowly, vigilantly, Vince crossed the bridge that hung over the highway. Stepping off it, he slipped and fell to one knee near a rock, his hands pressing against the leaf-covered ground. He got up slowly, checked to hear his mother's voice, then kept walking. Somewhere up ahead was his bench, where he yearned to rest for awhile. He took a few more steps, then saw the moonlight reflected on the water. With the pond in sight, he knew his bench was near; in fact, he appeared to be walking directly toward it. It was only when it seemed no more than a few yards away that he realized there were people on it who were having some form of sex. One appeared to be seated on the bench, the other standing. It was probably two men, but he couldn't be sure, their genders being erased in the dark. Vince began backpedaling, then turned around. "It's a good thing I saw that dog walker earlier or I would have been really startled," he thought, and it was a good thing in a way that the bench was occupied, since his purpose was to go to the field and he really had no time for rest or diversion.

He walked more quickly then. The voice was beginning to fade and he wanted to still be hearing it when he reached the field. The clearing grew wider, the moon more visible. He could feel the ground become smoother under his feet and knew he was finally in the field. At first he circled and walked across it several times. It was very quiet. There was no sign. He sat down in what he imagined was the center of the field and waited. The ground was cold and slightly wet and Vince closed his eyes tightly to re-capture the sense of his dream and his mother's voice.

Once, while he sat, he almost felt the ground give way and open up, could almost feel himself tunneling down to where his parents were wait-ing to embrace him in a world of light below the earth. But it didn't hap-pen. There were always signs like the feel and smell of the wet, bumpy ground that reminded him he had gone nowhere.

Sometime later, he gave up and began to walk toward his apartment. "So that's the park," Vince thought, "a place where dogs shit, people screw, and the dead make false promises to rejoin the living."

Still, when he was back in his room, in the half light of early morning, he missed the park and wished he had been there when he could have seen it in the daylight. After all, he had gone there on a mission filled with desperate hope. He shouldn't judge the park too harshly in light of those conditions. The park, itself, was not to blame, nor was there any point in trying not to see the park if he still saw it in his dreams. No point in keeping his blinds shut either and walking with his head down if he *thought* about the park while he was walking. It would be better to ac-knowledge it, to even walk through it every now and then, as he had an hour ago, as long as he divested it of its former significance. Yes, the key was not to believe that it had any special powers. The key was to simply let it be a park.

Twenty minutes later he got out of bed and opened the blinds in his bedroom, then in the living room and study. The park looked as it did in his dreams—immense, serene, and, under the pebble-pink patches in the early morning sky, slightly mysterious. He thought he would go to it after eating breakfast, perhaps before all the dogs and dog walkers got there. Later, thinking about the park so much, he had trouble reading Schopenhauer. He kept rereading the same paragraph, which no longer made any sense to him. In his mind he heard again, though faintly, his mother's voice from his last dream—"We're here. We're here." Then he grabbed his jacket and left his apartment, not even remembering to lock his door.

The elevator stopped three times before it reached the lobby. Four people got on. They seemed to ignore him but small-talked with each other. Small matter; he yearned to get to the park and hoped for no more delays. The doorman was not at his desk in the lobby as Vince walked as briskly as he could toward the door, nearly bumping into an elderly lady with a large bag of groceries who was standing outside the building by the doorway. She looked at him with slightly stunned, saucer eyes. He apologized, then realized she was waiting for the doorman to help her with her overly full grocery bag.

"Would you like some help with that bag?" he said. It wouldn't kill him to help this poor woman for a minute. She looked at him doubtfully. It had been a long time, if ever, since Vince had seen a person with such a vulnerable expression. Perhaps he had had such an expression in his eyes·when he first met Janice for lunch and it had scared her away.

"Oh thank you, so much. That's very kind of you. I'm afraid my shopping cart broke down . . . I wonder where Walter is," she said, referring to the doorman.

Vince opened the door, picked up the bag, and carried it to the elevator. It occurred to him that it would still be difficult for her to carry it into her apartment. The woman was so small and frail, and at least seventy years old. Now that she had opened her navy blue coat she was even skinnier than he realized. He asked her if he could bring the bundle to her apartment and she thanked him profusely and told him she lived on the eleventh floor—one floor above him.

"I wonder why I haven't seen you before," he said to her in the elevator. Her eyes were friendly looking now, he decided. They were warm and blue.

"I don't get out much, but I've seen you. You always looked like you were thinking about something."

"I guess I was."

The elevator door opened and he walked her to the door.

"Could I bring it in for you?"

"Why, thank you. You're being very nice," she said, fidgeting with her key. "Would you like a cup of tea?"

"Yes, thanks, I'd like that." He set the bundle down on the counter by her sink and began unpacking it and putting the perishables in her refrigerator. When he was finished, she thanked him again and invited him to sit at the table in her living room. Her apartment was filled with rose and green furniture and paintings. They were ordinary enough colors on the one hand, yet heavenly in a way because they were so appropriate to her life. He thought he could feel a part of her life in each piece of furniture. Her table was in the same place as his was, just in front of her long counter top. He noticed that her living room window also faced the park and turning his head he looked at it briefly. It was just a park. A pretty, though muted-looking, group of trees now that most of their leaves had fallen and their color gone. He sat down with his back to it. He was vaguely aware that he was smiling. The woman was wearing a blue dress that matched her coat and was smiling at him, too, as she brought in the tea and cookies.

"Well, we're here," she said. "I hope you like oatmeal cookies; I made them yesterday."

"Thanks, I do. I haven't had any homemade food in a long time."

She looked concerned for a moment. "Really? Well that's a shame. You're such a kind young man to help me the way you did. My name's Gertrude," she said, extending her skinny arm to shake hands with him.

He felt he was feeling the touch of destiny at last.

"I'm Vince," he said, smiling widely now and grasping her small hand in his.

MY SISTER'S HOUSE

There were rows of stairs, a waterfall of stairs, and I was
high up on one of them, yet there were many more above me. I was a
spectator in the house, which was also my house, but when you're a child
it's like being a small mushroom in a forest. It's your forest but you're
compelled to think of it as *the* forest that belongs to others, perhaps to
the trees.

Later I thought of the house as a castle that somehow included me. It
was white with twenty steep cement steps in two rows that led to the
black front door. The castle had four floors and twenty-one rooms including an outdoor patio surrounded by a gray cement wall, colored
stained-glass windows in the sunroom, and large eye-like oval-shaped
windows on the top floor through which it seemed one could survey the
entire activities of the town. From there I could see my friends on the
playground, friends whom I loved so dearly then though none of them
really lasted and by my mid-twenties were virtually all gone. The castle-
house had an ample front and back yard that were protected from the
street by two hills, one on each side of the stairs. Similarly, there were
fences and two rows of trees that shielded the entire length of the yard
from each neighbor.

It's the oddest thing. You are born into a kingdom and you spend the
rest of your life remembering it. That's what happened to my sister and
me. Only much later did we become detectives and try to understand
how the kingdom worked. All your archetypes are in the kingdom. Thus,

flowers will always mean the trellis roses and lilac trees that bloomed in our backyard and snow will always mean sledding down the hills of our front yard or down the alley in back.

Over this castle-house presided the King. Like all kings he had a paradoxical nature that mystified his subjects. He had a deep authoritative voice yet he was short, perhaps 5 feet, 6 inches. But so authoritative was his voice or demeanor that for many years I thought him to be much taller than he was, and years later my sister told me she thought the same thing. The King was from Norway and spoke with an accent, yet far from being an impediment this only contributed to his mystical aura. One couldn't really expect him to speak ordinary, uninflected English. The accent suited him, just as it suited him perfectly to speak six languages fluently and to ostensibly know everything about politics and philosophy.

The King was so many things—a renowned director and character actor, a distinguished cofounder of a theater who was honored nationally, and, of course, a towering figure in the Philadelphia theater world. He'd been a child prodigy who helped support his large family in Norway for years. He was also a man who endured unspeakable pain and isolation for twenty-seven years, between his first marriage and his final one to my mother. Surely that was endurance worthy of a god.

His contradictions were also deity-sized. He was a fervent Marxist who played the stock market and lived in a palace. He was an imposing man who inspired if not exactly terror then an ongoing low-level anxiety in me. Yet he was often surprisingly gentle and forgiving, as when he forgave me so easily for breaking one of the sunroom's stained glass windows with a baseball, or years later when he opened my door and saw me kissing my first girlfriend, whom I'd snuck into my room. He was able to joke about it with me that very night.

It was so different with my sister, Daneen. She never experienced the King's forgiveness simply because in his eyes she never did anything deviant enough to require it. Their communication was so close and harmonious that she soon learned to speak Norwegian from him. How she loved speaking in a foreign language which neither the Queen nor I understood! Like the King, my sister had a real gift for foreign languages and would have pursued that field I'm sure were there not one thing that pleased the old Commander even more, namely that she become a drama professor (which she did) where she could teach and eventually write about his work. So it was I alone who heard the King's disapproving words that shook my little mushroom soul, which perhaps was more like a wind-ripped leaf while he said them than a mushroom. I could only metamorphose from leaf to mushroom and resume my former place in the forest hours after his words had ceased. But later he might do something magnificently restorative where I would once more temporarily feel intact. Such was the case when he accompanied me to the playground to demand the basketball the big kids had taken from me. How frightened I was for him as we walked there. He was short (I suddenly realized for the first time) with gray hair—already over sixty years old—yet he walked right up to them, the delicate director/professor, with the accent which he lost only while performing and said, "I'll take the ball now," and they gave it to him without saying a word. That was my favorite memory of him except for a much earlier one where he stood over me, removing and then placing back a blanket over my shoulders, because I was too hot with it and too cold without it, until I was finally able to sleep.

Yes, my King could be brave and tender but he was always old. I remember lying in my bathtub calculating what age I'd be when he'd die. I'd read that the average life span of a man was seventy and concluded I'd be fourteen when it would happen. Whenever the telephone rang late at night or even in the afternoon when he was late arriving from the theater, I worried that it was the doctor in a hospital or else the police calling to inform us of his death.

But I'm making it seem as if the King dominated my life. The truth is he was often away traveling or absorbed in his work and did very few things alone with me. My sister, too, would tell me later that she often felt she was inventing him more than she was remembering him. That's one of the problems when you become a family detective, you think you want knowledge but your wishes interfere, so when the knowledge finally comes it's clouded. I want to see things in a balanced way now above all else, and kings can make you lose your balance. Actually queens can too. One of the first things I realized in my early years was that despite the vast power of the

King, it was she who decided when we would entertain and who we would invite. It was she who decided when we needed to hire or fire a maid, where we would go on our vacations, even which restaurants we would eat at or which movies we'd attend. (Alas, despite her talents as an actress, she was an inveterate fan of Hollywood kitsch.) Worst of all were her monumentally indiscreet stories, often sexually outrageous in content, sometimes teeming with not-so-subtle references to her own sexual frustration. (For years she and the King had lived in separate rooms.) But why did the King permit this? Why did he so rarely challenge her? It seemed a self-defeating way to show one's love, even if one were a king.

With the King away so much, I was left alone in the castle with the two women. To be with the Queen often meant lying in her bed while she rehearsed her lines but then getting to kiss her hundreds of times when she was through. She was soft and pretty and so funny, especially the way she could become other people. In her comic scenes she could make people laugh whenever she wanted and I laughed harder than anyone. But more often than not it also meant listening to the same stories about her dysfunctional and traitorous relatives or the dysfunctional and traitorous directors, actors, and critics who stabbed her in the back. As I got older it meant seeing how upset it made her to meet my girlfriends or any friends of mine at all. And when I got still older, long after the King had died, it meant learning that she'd betrayed the King once with an affair. She told me, after a few drinks, less than a year ago while I was visiting her in the Castle during Thanksgiving. (I was shocked at first but not really surprised since they'd lived in separate rooms all those years, and though I felt some sense of anger and hurt for the King I ultimately decided not to comment.)

My sister, on the other hand, liked to hear about my friends. She was four years older and competed against me in every sport, especially baseball and badminton and also in games like Chinese Checkers and Parcheesi. Her name was Daneen, but she wanted to be called Victor, appropriately enough. It was fun to beat her in the sports and games, as I often did, but I also felt bad when she'd pound her fist on the board and cry sometimes after losing. As I got older we began playing our own games together, inventing a group of characters and a kind of ongoing soap opera between them. Once my character kissed her character and a thrill unlike anything I'd ever felt surged through me.

My sister had a beautiful face and a full bosom that I admired but she didn't seem proud of her large breasts. She was always overweight, sometimes fat, consequently she didn't have many boyfriends or go to the dances in grammar school or high school, and the Queen worried out loud about her though the King never said a word against her. The King simply adored my sister, and one had to accept that.

One day I went into her room to sharpen my pencil and saw her naked in bed with one of her girlfriends from school.

"I just wanted to sharpen my pencil," I said, eyes straight ahead and aimed at the wall away from them, as soldier-like I sharpened the pencil, about-faced, and exited in a daze. I roamed the hallways, then up and down the waterfall stairs for countless hours. Finally I wandered into the Queen's room and she tearfully guessed what happened and tried to reassure me. The Queen's softness could be exquisite.

· · · · · · · · ·

Years passed. My sister and I moved away from the King and Queen, who continued to live in the Castle with the help of a series of live-in maids. (After the King died, a series of nurses were added, who continue to care for the Queen to this day.) I moved first to New York and then other states, wherever I could get a teaching job but my sister moved just a few miles from the Castle in Rosemont to an apartment in Philadelphia. I was no longer close to Daneen, though I wasn't sure why. During a visit to the Berkshires I bumped into her during the intermission of a play in Williamstown (at the theater the King and Queen had both been associated with), and when I went to hug her she turned away from me.

Meanwhile the King and Queen continued to prosper in their careers. Even after the King retired from the theater he cofounded he continued directing, sometimes plays that featured the Queen (she'd always been quasi-dependent on him professionally), well into his eighties. He was admired and beloved everywhere, it seemed. He'd been a fine chess player in his youth and people still loved to play with him. He inspired reverence among the chess players as he did with his former students who wrote or telephoned and often visited him from all over the country. He was a man who knew how to get along with people. Not so the Queen who lost best friend after friend because she thought they didn't sympathize with her or appreciate her enough. These breakups were horrible, like broken love affairs. Only her family didn't leave her. We were, all of us, including the paradoxically meek King, ultimately under her control. And ultimately in many ways I suppose I myself loved her more than I loved the King or anyone else.

· · · · · · · · · ·

When he was eighty-eight, the King had a stroke while playing chess and died three months later in a hospital. At the memorial in the Walnut Street Theatre in Philadelphia a number of celebrated theater people spoke. The King's accomplishments as a director, actor, and theater-owner were all reviewed. One of his colleagues referred to him as a noble man. He'd helped so many young actors and directors, he was honest, selfless—all of which, I suppose, added up to noble.

At the memorial I read a poem about him, which along with a variation of it remain the only poems I have ever written. After the ceremony my sister told me she was touched by it and we experienced a moment of closeness again before returning to our separate lives. In many ways her fate mirrored mine. We both wrote, or tried to; my sister eventually wrote a whole book about the King's life in the theater but neither of us, of course, could support ourselves by writing the way the King and Queen supported themselves by their art. We were both teachers (an apt profession for the truly dominated) who lived alone. She was simply more successful at it, getting tenure in her drama department long before I got it as a musicologist. There was no particular shortage of women that we could sleep with but neither of us had children. When we talked on the phone we talked almost exclusively about the Queen. It was that way for years. Meanwhile, the Queen's ailments were increasing exponentially. Despite inheriting virtually all of the King's money, she was reluctant to spend any of it, even on her health. Her fears of her childhood poverty recurring were worse than ever, as was her ability to listen to others—now that she was half deaf, the one physical problem she had that she wouldn't acknowledge. Yes, there was a lot to talk about as my annual visit to my sister's house approached in the summer of my forty-fifth year.

Something else. I'd developed an interest, that began a number of months ago, in Margo, a homeless black woman who lived on my block in Boston not too far from the school where I finally got tenure. She looked to be somewhere in her middle thirties and was pretty and quite fastidious. She spent a great deal of her time on her makeup and wore bright red lipstick. She was also neat with her belongings and the cardboard box she slept in. Occasionally she ranted a bit, but most often she was warm and extroverted in a friendly way. I talked to Margo at least every other day and gave her about fifteen dollars a week.

The last few weeks I'd wanted her to visit my apartment and had invited her several times. She laughed each time and said with a quasi-Caribbean accent, "You want to add some dark meat to your plate, sir, is that it? Oh no, I don't think so sir," or other words like that. I assured her that wasn't the case but when I was with myself I wondered what I did want. I'd been lonely lately and enjoyed Margo's company, and I did have a desire to give her a good dinner and have her sit on my relatively comfortable furniture and take a long bath if she wanted. Certainly, I wouldn't have minded eventually having some kind of physical contact with her, if she initiated it. I knew I'd never force myself on her, my sexual ego being far too fragile for anything like that. But, yes, I did wonder about her sexually and even fantasized about having a child with her from time to time. At any rate, I reassured her that sex was not my goal, that I simply enjoyed her company.

"You stay in front of my building; don't you want to be inside it once? Watch some TV, listen to music, hang out for a while?"

She laughed again. "Your money is fine sir, I don't need your house."

That line made me laugh, too, it was delivered so well. She had a gift for banter and I enjoyed the fact that our relations were light and pleasant, so I didn't press her too much. At last there was a woman in my life with whom things could be friendly and humorous. It was the very opposite of what awaited me in the Berkshires, where I'd undoubtedly be engaged in a long, intensely painful dialogue with my sister about the Queen's failing health and what exactly we should or could do about it.

It was the certain knowledge that that was what was in store for me that made me ask Margo if she wouldn't like to accompany me there. After all, I knew that Jean, my sister's girlfriend, would be in the house and that she always stayed with my sister whenever I visited. If my sister could use Jean as a buffer, why must I visit my sister alone?

"Wouldn't you like to go to the country?" I asked Margo. "My sister has a pool that overlooks the mountains."

"Oh my God, no," she said smiling. "It's fine here where I can overlook the alley and other people in their boxes and know that I have the cleanest, best-looking box in Boston. That's good enough for me, sir," she said quasi-sarcastically.

There was no point pursuing my idea further, I decided, so a week later I got on the bus for the interminable ride that took me to Stockbridge where my sister was waiting for me in her new red sports car. We exchanged a rather awkward hug and then sped away on the road to her house in Interlaken.

One big difference between my sister and me is that because she got tenure well before I did she was able to stay in Philadelphia essentially her whole life. She's moved only once that I recall, from one apartment in Philadelphia to another, and then four years ago managed to buy her country house not far from the Stockbridge Theater, where the King and Queen once performed. Her house is large and roomy and filled with pictures and memorabilia about the King. (There he is with his arm around John Gielgud. There he is at a party with Edward Albee and Tennessee Williams.) Tiger lilies and other wildflowers grow around her house and in the backyard, which slopes uphill steeply to the pool. Behind the pool is a badminton court, a gazebo, and a fine view of the hills.

I, on the other hand, have been the proverbial gypsy scholar, moving from one part of the country to another—wherever there was work. As a result, there was never a real chance for me to buy a house, and I've lived exclusively in a series of one-room apartments. These apartments were never spectacularly bad to live in, incidentally, yet each had an Achilles heel of a kind that really was quite horrific. Even in my current post-tenure apartment, which has two bedrooms and to which I've often invited Margo, there's a bad problem in the bathroom where, due to a running faucet, a small window, poor ventilation, and decaying plaster, a tropical rain forest level of humidity has developed and a mushroom-like fungus has actually begun blooming near my bathroom mirror.

In the car I asked my sister two questions. "How about this new car?" was question one.

She smiled. "You like it?"

"It's very chic. How do you afford it so soon after buying the house?"

"You know me, I'm a spender. I have nothing in the bank." That's true. She's like the King that way, whereas as I've gotten older I've become more of a horder like the Queen.

I laughed, "Where's Jean?" was my other question. My sister answered that Jean was reading by the pool. So Jean has granted us this private moment, I thought. I didn't expect there to be many more. Jean has blondish, slightly graying hair and intense eyes like my sister and is also an academic, but there the similarity ends. While Jean is more outgoing and has a more charming social presentation of self, I suppose (which has helped her a lot professionally as an administrator), she's also much more controlling and possessive than my sister. Jean generally makes sure she and my sister stay close to each other in most social situations, and I was surprised my sister had ventured forth to meet me alone. Looking out the window at the trees and hills, I wondered if that meant anything special, but there was no sign of it during the rest of the ride home.

· · · · · · · · ·

Jean was by the pool, as advertised. She exchanged a minute's worth of pleasantries with me before returning to the newspaper she was reading on a chaise lounge. I sat in a chair neither too near nor far away from her. It was strange. Having thought so intensely about my family on the bus trip, I suddenly couldn't stop thinking about Jean. It was as if my mind seized upon the chance to think about someone else and wouldn't let go. I thought about how I never knew whether to hug Jean when I saw her or not and ended up never even touching her. Then I thought about how Jean and my sister never touch in public and how I've never seen them touch in private either. When Jean and Daneen fell in love, Jean was married with two young children. For the next seven years she stayed married, living a double life with Daneen, who had to accept that Jean was regularly sleeping with her husband and that she had to pose as a mere friend of their mother's when she was with Jean's children, to whom she got quite attached. It took Jean twenty-three years to finally, partially, come out of the closet. She divorced her husband much earlier, of course, but still kept up a kind of heterosexual pretense. Even now it still isn't clear to me what she's told her children about my sister.

I'd have to say, though, that in spite of all the unusual circumstances, both of Jean's children turned out well. I don't know Louise as well, though I hear about her various successes in business, but Phil is a charming, funny man with a good starting-out job in a law firm. He's married to a quite attractive woman who just got pregnant, and both he and Louise appear to have excellent relationships with their mother. They joke, they respect each other, there's nothing overtly possessive or neurotic between them. Not that Jean is without her faults, but as a parent she appears to be Supermom. I give her all the credit in the world for that, though lately I've felt a pang of envy when I see her with her kids and also some resentment when I watch my sister cater to her every whim. Meanwhile, my sister was like a second mother to Jean's children, without her having any of her own. Of course, Daneen could have had children despite her sexual preference. She even has lesbian friends who did it with a sperm donation from a gay friend and a turkey baster with quite happy results. I think my sister wanted to have a child, or at least part of her did, but something in her feared it too and so she ultimately didn't. To be around Jean, then, is a constant reminder for both my sister and me of our childlessness and all that that means. Rationalize it as you will, but for most people if you don't have children by a certain age it's like having a permanent wound that the world manages to irritate every day.

At this gloomy and dramatic moment in my thought progression my sister suddenly emerged from the house in her bathing suit. She didn't see me at first since her slightly worried look was directed wholly at Jean. I was a mere mushroom again for the next few moments, lost among the tiger lilies. "Hi Daniel," she said, without waving when she did see me, and I tried with my usual lack of success not to stare at her large, still youthful-looking breasts.

Although my sister has always been overweight, she's always been very athletic. She is not a person, even at forty-nine, to spend much time sitting by a pool. She sat next to Jean for a couple of minutes, then got up and made a graceful dive into the pool, which made me remember that she was on her college swimming team. A minute later, I got up from my chair and went into the water myself. My sister had been doing a vigorous backstroke and for a minute or so we were in the water together. Then Jean began reading a review of last night's concert from *The Berkshire Eagle* and Daneen stopped swimming to listen. Soon both women were laughing and hooting with glee as they discovered that the review agreed exactly with their low assessment of the piano soloist and the guest conductor.

I got on one of the floats, as my sister left the pool to sit next to Jean, and paddled off into a far corner. I was thinking about how many chances to have children I've had in my life. It's strange that I've been reviewing this intermittently in my mind the last few years, since it's not as if the number's changed and it's not as if it's a great and complicated number to remember. I define a real chance to have a child as the conscious attempt by each partner to do it even if (as in my case) that conscious attempt happened only once or twice before a change of heart or a breakup or abortion occurred. My total number of chances has been seven for some time. If a TV drama were made of my life I think they should call me, and the show, "Daniel Seven," a name both catchy and symbolic like the old "Peter Gunn" show. Floating around in the pool, looking up at the tops of the tiger lilies and the hills in the distance, and at an unusually bright blue Berkshire sky almost the same color as my sister's bathing suit, I actually wondered if Henry Mancini, the "Peter Gunn" theme composer, were still alive so he could write the theme for "Daniel Seven," and then when I realized what I'd been thinking about I started to laugh. Jean said, "What's so funny Danny? I could use a laugh." But, of course, I said nothing about it, which made Daneen say, "He's always been secretive."

At dinner the usual conversational pattern prevailed. It began with Jean and me praising my sister's roast beef, then got into fairly light-hearted shop talk, though not without some edge to it, because like most academics they were angry about their lot. I was angry too, but no longer bothered to talk about it. Inevitably, there was a political argument, as if the anger having been aroused by shop-talk foreplay had to climax in a more important forum. These discussions made me uneasy because my sister was so excitable, and I feared her temper when she got excited. She would pound the table, sometimes, like she did as a child, or yell, and her face would contort in a fearsome way. When she drank, as she did that night, it made such outbursts all the more likely. To top if off, Jean made a joke about lesbians. My sister is very sensitive about women jokes in general and lesbian ones in particular, and not wanting to witness her reaction I got up from the table, saying I had to go to the bathroom. I did, in fact, go to the bathroom, not to use it but to hide from the conversation. On the way there I was struck by how few photographs of the King were left in the house. What had happened? My sister's house looked almost naked with so few images of the old Commander and I felt as if she'd somehow betrayed him.

I never did discover what the argument was about, something to do with Newt and Candice Gingrich. It was like listening for an explosion of thunder after first hearing some vague rumblings. But the thunder didn't come. Daneen surprised me by not erupting. I returned to the table and it was like the calm after a storm, except that the storm never happened. It was true there was still more tension in the air than usual, but fortunately there was a concert at Tanglewood to go to which we all had to get dressed for. The concert soon became the focus of all our discussion and energy and, as it turned out, it rewarded us well. When we got back home we all agreed it had been a fine performance and that we were all tired now, and so the first day at my sister's house ended without any real catastrophe.

· · · · · · · · · ·

I was extraordinarily tired the next morning. Despite sleeping a long time, I stayed in my room longer than usual. I'd had a disturbing dream the night before in which I saw the King talking very intensely and privately with Margo. It was as if even in my dreams (and from beyond the grave) the old Commander was still controlling my life with women.

When I finally left my room I heard some strange sounds—a combination of half-muffled crying and talking coming from my sister's room. They're probably making love or having a quarrel, I thought, or possibly combining them, so let it be. But the little sneak in me couldn't ignore it. Dedicated family detective that I was I tiptoed down the hallway to get closer to the door, fully aware of how absurdly comical I would have looked if anyone had seen me. I didn't listen long and I didn't hear much. There was an exchange that sounded like, "It happened again."

"What?"

"I remembered again."

Then I didn't hear anything intelligible except for the crying sound until two minutes later when Jean said, "Does Daniel know?" at which point I instantly began to feel more guilty than curious and started back-pedaling on my tiptoes as if I were executing an awkward ballet step.

That morning incident was on the edge of my mind all day, though Daneen seemed cheerful enough. Yet I had the feeling that she was acting. This was especially disturbing since I thought of her as belonging to the emotionally nontheatrical part of my family, along with the King.

That night they invited me to go to the movies with them. They'd had enough of high culture and wanted to see a "fun" movie that was playing in Pittsfield. Having my father's aversion to movies, however, I said I wanted to go to the concert instead, so they dropped me off at Tanglewood.

There was a short Haydn symphony, and then the romantic part of the program began. Prokofiev's Third Piano Concerto followed by Tchaikovsky's Sixth—two pieces that capture the very essence of bittersweet love. But I didn't think of any of my past loves as I thought I might and I didn't think much about having a baby either. Instead my mind fastened on my sister's remark about me that she'd made in the pool the day before—"He's so secretive." It was said jokingly, but it was also meant as a true observation, one she'd said intermittently over the years. It hurt me to hear it, though I could hardly deny it was true. But how, I kept wondering during both concerto and symphony, could I have become any other way, living as I did in such a house full of secrets, a house that made me a perpetual detective of my own family?

Then I remembered that last summer I'd seen some odd notes on the writing table by my sister's bed describing something erotic while using the pronoun "he." Perhaps that's how she thought of Jean—I didn't want to know at the time, having wandered in merely to talk to my sister. So I left the room and more or less blocked out the notes, which were definitely in Daneen's writing. Yes, it was a house full of secrets. There was my sister hiding her attraction to girls as she grew up, and there were the King and Queen living in different rooms. There was also the King's otherworldly harmony with my sister compared to which his kindness toward *me* had an almost guilty or forced quality, and then after years of closeness my sister literally turning away from me. There was also the sudden disappearance of the King's photographs from her house and, finally, her strange notes and Jean's asking, "Does Daniel know?" Know what, of course, was the question.

By the end of the concert I felt an urgent need to talk alone with her but it was impossible. When she and Jean picked me up they were telling dirty jokes and making fun of the movie and were very much in their inseparable mode. During the ride I suddenly wanted to say, "Why don't you two kiss or at least put your arms around each other? You're obviously in the mood and you know that I've known about you two for twenty-five years." But, of course, it didn't happen. Reticence and secrecy were still their way.

. . . .

"Do you want to play badminton?" I suddenly said to Daneen late the next afternoon while Jean was napping in a chaise lounge by the pool. My sister hesitated for a moment, perhaps wondering if it would disturb Jean, or perhaps she was simply surprised that I casually suggested doing something we'd last done so long ago. But she agreed and when she returned with the rackets there was a smile on her face. Almost immediately we began slamming the birdie back and forth just like we did thirty-five years ago, still pretty evenly matched. We didn't play a game, though I was keeping a kind of unofficial score in my mind and felt she was, too. What a woman, I thought, while she was playing. To be a college professor of drama and to appreciate music and to be so good at sports! No wonder the

King loved her so much; no wonder she couldn't find her niche with other men who were so vulgar and limited by comparison. She was too good for them, she was too good, generally speaking, for the male sex and had to be with women, I thought, just as I broke my racket while hitting a vicious overhead. For a moment we both stood stunned at the sight of the birdie wedged in the space where the strings spread slightly too far apart and then we started to laugh. They were cheap rackets, so we could afford to laugh about it. We sat down on two chairs by the pool, breathing heavily, as was Jean, who was still asleep. Then a minute later the laughter seemed a part of the distant past as we began talking about the Queen.

"I've noticed a real difference in her the last month or so. She's not the same person anymore," my sister said, pushing two locks of blondish, light brown hair away from her eyes. It occurred to me that she had approximately the same color hair and eyes as I did and that we also shared the same general facial shape.

"What do you mean?" I said, although I did know what she meant.

"It's like she's crossed over into another world."

"You're exaggerating, tremendously exaggerating."

"No, Daniel, I don't think so. Her depression, her denial of what's happening to her. Her complete unwillingness to face reality."

"What reality?"

"The reality that she'll never walk again, that she'll have to spend the rest of her life in a wheelchair. No matter how often the doctors tell her, she doesn't believe them or accept it."

"She's probably not even hearing them. The one thing that *has* gotten worse is her hearing, but, of course, she's far too vain to ever acknowledge that and get a hearing aid. She'd rather not hear a single word you or I say the rest of her life than admit she needs a hearing aid."

"It isn't that. She does know what the doctors say. But when they tell her what the situation is she simply sees another doctor and continues believing what she wants to believe. The woman survives, has always survived, by believing what she needs to."

"What do you mean?" I asked, but she didn't answer me.

"The thing that really worries me," she continued, "is that she's in real danger living at home with these nurses coming in different shifts. The reality is she's alone too long every day and her vertigo is worse now and when she tries to walk, even with the walker, there's always the chance that she'll have another serious fall. What she needs is constant, supervised care in some kind of place where that care exists."

"You mean a nursing home? She'll never do that. Her whole life is in her home. Her career, her memories. Katharine Hepburn was in that house. She'll never let that happen."

"The point is the time may come, may already have come, when that has to happen."

"In the name of what?" I said excitedly, suddenly feeling tremendously protective of the Queen.

"In the name of saving her life. I'd like to feel you'll be my ally if and when that happens."

I didn't say anything to that. I stayed silent while my sister talked some more about it. I was chastened, diminished. I was a mushroom again among the giant trees that shaded my sister's pool. I might have left it at that—I was never as good or as relentless an arguer as Daneen—but apparently there was still some adrenaline residue in me from the badminton match. I let her finish about how we would have to be allies in all things concerning our mother. I conceded the point, knowing that my blunt sister was correct again, and then I changed the subject. I asked her why there were so few photographs of the King in her home now? In fact, as I asked the question I couldn't remember seeing one. A strange look swept over my sister's face and I knew I'd not only caught her off guard but hit a nerve, as well.

"I find it especially odd when I remember what your house was like last summer. I mean it used to be like a shrine for him."

"I went overboard with that," she said. "I got a little carried away and so I stopped. Don't you think we've both been too overwhelmed by our parents for too long?"

"What do you mean?" I said, knowing, of course, what she meant.

"That we've been so caught up in their lives it's kept us from doing some things we wanted to."

"What things?"

"Having children, for instance. You told me once you wanted to."

"True enough."

"So? It's too late for me but maybe you should do something about it. I know you'd be a good father. I'm sure you'd honor that."

Again I changed the subject, not wanting to be sidetracked from my investigation.

"I heard some crying this morning, you know, by accident. Was that you?"

I sensed Daneen would be looking away from me, and not wanting to see that I looked past her at the still sleeping Jean.

"Yes, that was me," my sister said, half-looking at the ground. "I didn't know it was that loud."

"I just heard it for a few seconds in the hall, but, of course, I was concerned. I heard my name mentioned, too."

"What did you hear?"

"Something like, 'Does Daniel know?' So naturally I wondered if I'd done something to upset you."

"No, nothing like that."

"I mean you must admit we've had a kind of strange history."

"How so?"

"We were so close growing up and then I always felt you turned away from me somewhere in your twenties and I didn't have that much contact with you after that until a few years ago, so I don't want anything to go wrong now. I'm touchy about that."

"Nothing's gone wrong with us," she said, but she looked slightly nervous.

"I guess I always wondered what went wrong all those years ago, why we . . ."

"We were too close then, almost incestuously close, and I just couldn't handle it. It was hard enough deciding to be a full-fledged lesbian. And it was a lot harder to be one then than it is now, believe me. Not that it's so easy now. Look, do you really want to talk about this?"

"Yes."

"Then let's go inside. I need a drink, and . . ." She gestured toward Jean and I nodded and began to follow Daneen down the stone steps that were cut into her lawn.

It was like descending a waterfall. As soon as I went down two steps I felt a curious shortening of space. There was nothing but my sister and me, the trees around us having blurred like watercolors. We sat across the table in her kitchen. A dragonfly was hitting its head against the window. It had to do with the King, did I want to hear? She'd been wondering for some time if she should tell me but she guessed she should because it had to do with a lot of my questions she supposed—why she turned away from me and men in general, though, yes, she'd always liked women more, but she'd liked men, too, for a while, should she go on? I nodded. It was chaos, her words, but I expected that in the beginning. I was on a cataract of water and sat still at the table to hold on.

At first, when she thought of it, it was like dreams, or rather she turned the memories into dreams, though it still affected her and made her repulsed by men for a while. That was in her middle twenties. Then it went away.

"What? What went away?" I said.

Then she told me. It was like a roaring in my ear. Like human yelling in a mushroom ear. It was so loud that I didn't hear even as she said it again. She told me next that her mind found a way to keep it away such a large percentage of the time that when it did happen she could dismiss it as a fantasy or a new way of punishing herself. But last summer it came back during my visit. She guessed she identified me with him, she said, and in spite of everything, for a moment I couldn't help feeling proud to remind someone of the King.

But the roar came back, stuck with me this time, and I focused more clearly. "How bad was it?" I blurted.

Maybe not what you think, she said. There was no intercourse. She didn't even know if any orgasms were involved. Not hers, anyway, though she used to think about him during sex with men. She used to think about him all the time. She was afraid to think about anyone else. But with him, no intercourse, no penetration. Just a lot of fondling and touching in "bad places."

I felt myself shake inside. I felt curiously light and hollow. "When was this?" I said.

"He waited until I was a teenager," my sister said. She said it was shortly after he and the Queen started living in different rooms. That's when the Queen had her affair, I thought to myself, though I didn't say it, still didn't know if my sister knew that or not.

"You say that with a lot of sympathy," I finally said to her.

"His first wife hurt him and then his second wife did, too," she said quickly. He could master a lot of things but not that. Love, sex, it was like water in his hands, he couldn't control it, he nearly drowned in it, like a waterfall over his head.

"You don't even hate him, do you?"

"No. It was the worst of him, not all of him. Remember he was incredibly kind to me, to all of us most of the time."

"You still sympathize with him, don't you? Even now."

"Don't you? I can't help it. It was only for a year or part of a year, and it wasn't that many times. I mean, of course it was awful and I hated it. I'm not trying to minimize it. But it wasn't all of him, it wasn't the whole story, and I know he suffered a lot and felt enormously guilty."

"Christ," I said, interrupting. "Why did he do it?"

He was alone, she said. After the Queen's affair he changed. So you knew, I said. Yes, she knew. That's what changed him, she thought. He lost himself. It was no excuse, of course.

"Jesus Christ," I said.

"He'd get tears in his eyes every time," she said, with tears in her own eyes.

"It's probably why he never criticized you. He treated you like a goddamn princess, the hypocrite."

Then I noticed that she was crying softly, but I couldn't let up and I asked her if the Queen knew.

"I don't know. I can't be sure, she's such an actress."

"Did he tell you not to tell her, did he threaten you?" As if I could do anything about it, as if the King hadn't been dead for thirteen years.

"Yes, no. He didn't threaten anything, but he said it was part of our secret world and he'd ask me not to tell."

Christ. The thought of the King talking that way. "Christ," I said.

"Yes, Christ . . . Danny? Are you all right? Danny are you all right? It was very hard to tell you this."

"Yes, I'm all right. I'm sorry for you, that's all."

She thanked me. She said she loved me and told me she meant what she said about my being a good father. I told her about Margo, then, maybe to try to lighten things up a little. I said it quickly in a half-joking way, although my hand was still trembling. But my sister listened seriously, before encouraging me to try to meet women I'd have more in common with background-wise. Suddenly there were tears in my eyes too. I was still shocked in one way but not shocked in another. The oddest thing. Like all my detective work was a sham, a game I played with myself because I always half-knew.

Then I hugged my sister. She was shaking. I said, "Maybe you should be with Jean now," meaning maybe you want to be with Jean. She nodded and fell out of my embrace. I sat at the table. The dragonfly was gone. I watched Daneen climb the steps one by one. The trees came back into view. But before she got a quarter of the way to the pool Jean met her on the stone stairs. I watched my sister talk to her. I watched the two long-time lovers talking. My sister put her arm around Jean and I watched them hug each other. I saw the tiger lilies, the other flowers, the high trees. Then I looked around myself at the table and chairs and at the paintings on the walls. Everything had an order to it; everything seemed to sparkle that second in my sister's house.

Acknowledgments

"My Black Rachmaninoff" first appeared in *Ontario Review;* "Fear of Blue Skies" in *Shenandoah;* "Ghost Parks" in *Tampa Review;* "Mercury" in *Santa Barbara Review;* "Brook" and "Bodysurfing" in *Witness;* "Barry and Elliot" and "My Sister's House" in *Confrontation;* "The Towel" and "Mistakes" in *Triquarterly;* and "The Park" in *River Styx.*

I wish to express my gratitude to the following people who helped make this book possible: Tom Bevan, Richard and Julia Galligan Breslin, Valerie Dixon, Julia Hanna, Valerie Hanson, and Linda K. Harris.

Library of Congress Cataloging-in-Publication Data

Burgin, Richard.
    Fear of blue skies / Richard Burgin.
        p.   cm. — (Johns Hopkins, poetry and fiction)
    ISBN 0-8018-5745-7 (alk. paper)
    I. Title. II. Series.
PS3552.U717F42   1998
813'.54—dc21   97-21604
                                          CIP